P

MAX MAGIC

'Max Magic is the best book I've ever read. It's so funny and I love learning all the magic tricks too!'

Marlow, aged 10

'A great story to share with children to help inspire them to follow their dreams, and, importantly, to never give up.'

Teach Primary

'Fabulous fun-filled, great for all ages'

★★★★★

'A hit!'

★★★★★

'I loved the way Max and his friends stood up to Bottley and other bullies. Trying out the different magic tricks was great fun too. I give it 5 stars.'

Evie, aged 7

MAX MAGIC

THE INCREDIBLE HOLIDAY HIDEOUT

The Max Magic series

Max Magic

The Greatest Show on Earth

MAX MAGIC

THE INCREDIBLE HOLIDAY HIDEOUT

STEPHEN MULHERN

with TOM EASTON ♠ illustrated by
Begoña Fernández Corbalán

Piccadilly
PRESS

For Chippy. – T.E.

First published in Great Britain in 2024 by
PICCADILLY PRESS
4th Floor, Victoria House, Bloomsbury Square, London WC1B 4DA
Owned by Bonnier Books, Sveavägen 56, Stockholm, Sweden
bonnierbooks.co.uk/PiccadillyPress

The right of Stephen Mulhern, Tom Easton and Begoña Fernández Corbalán
to be identified as authors and illustrator of this work has been asserted by
them in accordance with the Copyright, Designs and Patents Act 1988.

This is a work of fiction. Names, places, events and incidents are either
the products of the author's imagination or used fictitiously. Any
resemblance to actual persons, living or dead, is purely coincidental.

A CIP catalogue record for this book is available from the British Library.

ISBN: 978-1-80078-384-3
Signed edition ISBN: 978-1-80078-810-7
Also available as an ebook and in audio

1

Typeset in Easy Reading Pro

EasyReading® Font
High-legibility typeface

Interior design by Nigel Baines. Illustrations by Begoña Fernández Corbalán
Inside cover illustrated doodles © Shutterstock
Author photograph © @Oliver_Rosser // @FeastCreative
Printed and bound in Great Britain by Clays Ltd, Elcograf S.p.A.

MIX
Paper | Supporting
responsible forestry
FSC® C018072
www.fsc.org

Piccadilly Press is an imprint of Bonnier Books UK
bonnierbooks.co.uk

Hello,

First of all, thank you so much for taking
the time to read my new book.

Also thank you for following Max on his
unbelievable journeys. I hope you are ready
to start reading about his third adventure!

Max Magic has only become so
magical because of YOU.

Always remember to believe that anything is
possible, and even when times are tough or you
feel a little sad, the show must go on!

No dream is ever too big and trust me,
you can make them come true.

AND FOR TODAY'S SHOW, MEET YOUR STARS . . .

MAX

LUCKY

DAISY

STRETCH

SOPHIE

SUSIE

VINNY

BARRY CRAYFISH

GARY CRAYFISH

PC PEACEFUL

1

The Show Must Go On

I woke with a groan.

It was the morning after the day after the night before.

Just thirty-six hours ago I'd been on a floodlit, noisy stage, surrounded by my friends and my family and a load of TV cameras. There was a cheering crowd

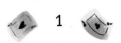 1

and dancers leaping about the stage. The nation's sweetheart, Willow Holloughby, had kissed me. TV's Fox Blackshaw had clapped me on the back. I had been on a high. After the dramatic confrontation with Mr Mysterio, I had been full of adrenaline, crackling and fizzing with magical power.

It was everything I'd always wanted. Glamour. Excitement. Attention.

Magic!

But Sunday had gone in a blur and now that feeling was over. The adrenaline was gone, the fizz had gone flat, the cake had gone stale. And I felt tired and sad.

I knew that things had worked out for the best. Dance troupe Inclusivity had deserved to win The Greatest Show on Earth, and there were more important things than winning competitions, receiving £10,000 in prize money and having your picture in the papers.

But right now, I couldn't quite remember what those other important things were.

I groaned again. Lucky looked up at me groggily.

'I'm trying to sleep,' he said with a growl. And I mean he quite literally **said** it, in a growly voice. Lucky is my dog. And he can talk. To me, at least. Everyone else just hears barks or growls or yips. Don't ask me how it works!

 3

What made it all worse was knowing that
if I had used my magic – I mean, my **real**
magic – I would have won the competition
hands down, feet up, one arm behind my
back, blindfolded and stuck head first in a
barrel of eels.

Because I possess **real, genuine** magical
abilities. A few weeks ago, I found an

old chest in the back room of my gran's antique shop in the East End of London. I opened it, and was hit with a crackle of power and a bright light. I ended up with a bump on the head. That wasn't the only thing I ended up with though. When my head stopped spinning, I found I had new powers: telekinesis, telepathy, and the casting of illusions. And recently I went back again and got one more power: the power of mind control.

My powers had got me and my friends out of some sticky spots. (And, if I'm honest, had got us **into** some sticky spots too.) But I had learned not to use them just to benefit myself or my family. The

times I'd tried that, I'd found myself in the stickiest spots of all.

To use my real magical abilities in a talent competition would have been cheating. And Max the Magnificent doesn't cheat. People like Mr Mysterio cheat. Or Bottley the Bully, or the Crayfish Twins.

But not me. I'm trying to be a nice guy. And maybe nice guys don't always finish last, but they don't usually finish first either.

Lucky got up, stretched, then leaped on top of me. 'Come on then, Max,' he said. 'It's a beautiful day.'

'It would be more beautiful if I had £10,000,' I said.

 6

'Never mind that,' he replied. 'You've got to get over the fact you lost the competition. The show must go on.'

'The show is over,' I grumbled.

'The show is **never** over,' he said. 'Now come and get breakfast.'

'I don't want breakfast.'

'I meant, come and get breakfast for **me**,' he said, jumping down and waiting by the door, wagging his little tail.

When I came downstairs, I was greeted by the usual chaos. I had been so sure I was going to win The Greatest Show on Earth, I had imagined the following days panning out very differently. I would be greeted by my adoring siblings, faces full

 7

of pride and admiration. My dad would offer me a plate of sausages and eggs. Mum would be counting out £50 notes on the dresser, all our financial troubles over.

The phone would be ringing and pinging like crazy with offers of gigs from magic theatres, TV companies, publishers with book deals. Newspaper and TV reporters would be on the doorstep, shouting extremely personal questions through the letter box.

But no. There was to be none of that.

Breakfast was a nearly empty box of shredded wheat and a thimbleful of milk. Dad was on the phone to his toy supplier, who was late with an order, apparently.

Mum was counting final demand bills on the dresser, sighing heavily. My sister and my brothers ignored me completely. The phone wasn't ringing. There was no one at the door except a delivery driver who'd got the wrong address.

This is what happens when you come second.

'At least I have you to talk to about it,' I said to Lucky as we walked to Gran's shop. Lucky stayed with Gran during the day while I was at school and everyone else was at work. 'You understand my pain.'

'Bongo the Labrador has been here,' Lucky said, sniffing a lamppost. 'And unless I'm very much mistaken, so has Mr Pip

 9

the Cockerpoo. I don't think he's drinking enough water.'

'Are you even listening to me?' I asked with a frown.

'What?' Lucky said. 'Oh, no, no. I rarely do, in fact.'

'I'm trying to explain to you how devastated I am,' I said, feeling hurt. 'My entire future has been thrown into doubt. The universe has been knocked off its axis and I'm swimming in the dark void of uncertainty.'

'Max,' Lucky said. 'You came second in a talent show. The act that came first was amazing. It's not like you've been denied your birthright as the heir to the throne and been sent into exile. You'll be **fine**.'

'You just don't understand.' I sighed.

'I understand you're being a drama queen,' Lucky said, walking on.

If I'd thought Gran might offer some consolation, I was wrong.

When I got to the shop, she'd just had a delivery of some old furniture. A couple of chairs, a set of nesting tables and a wardrobe. She waved at me and gave a brief smile, but to be honest she seemed a bit preoccupied. Lucky trotted over to her. Gran was wearing her favourite dress – the yellow one with black spots.

'Hi, Gran,' I said, trying to communicate just how sad I was through my flat tone.

 11

Usually I'm bright and bubbly. Effervescent, my friends might say. Ebullient, my parents might say. Extremely irritating, my siblings might say.

Gran bent down slowly to scratch Lucky's ear, wincing a little as she did so. I knew her back had been causing her pain, or 'Michael Caine' as she put it in Cockney rhyming slang. She bent and scratched Lucky's ear. 'Hello, boy,' she said absently, still frowning at the new old furniture.

'What about me?' I asked.

'Sorry, Max,' Gran said with a grin, apparently realising that she hadn't greeted me properly. She walked over and scratched me behind my ear as well.

'Not even a coin back there?' I asked with an eye roll.

She chuckled. 'No coins today. But you might get a kick out of this.' She moved back to the old wardrobe, which stood right in the middle of the shop floor. She opened the door and climbed in, pulling the door closed behind her.

'What are you doing?' I asked. 'Gran, be careful.'

Then the door opened and out she came. But her yellow dress with black spots had gone. She was now wearing a blue dress with red stripes.

'How did you do that?' I asked, astonished.

She wagged a finger. 'If I reveal how the magic is done, they'll throw me out of the Magic Circle.' She frowned. 'Again.'

'I didn't know you were in the Magic Circle,' I said. 'And I also didn't know you'd been thrown out of it.'

'There's a lot you don't know about me,' she said with a wink.

'Gran,' I said, 'when you and Grandpa used to go onstage and do your magic shows, did you ever feel a bit, well, down afterwards?'

Lucky jumped up into his favourite old armchair, settling down for a solid eight hours of sleep before I came to collect him that evening.

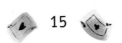

'Of course,' Gran said. 'When you're in showbiz, you get a buzz from being up onstage in front of hundreds of people who love what you do. With the lights shining in your face. The smell of the crowd and the roar of the greasepaint. When you know what it feels like to see people laughing and cheering in total amazement, it's only natural to feel like you've lost something once it's over.'

'But I really did lose something,' I said. 'Ten thousand somethings.'

'Is that what this is about?' Gran asked. 'Money?'

'Not just that,' I said. 'I thought I was going to find fame and fortune. I thought that finally I was going to be Max the Magnificent. That I'd get to the tippermost of the toppermost!'

'My advice is: don't get to the top too early,' Gran said. 'Nowhere to go except down again. And on the way back down you meet all the people you've annoyed.'

I sighed and slumped into an old armchair, raising a cloud of dust.

'Did you have any training?' I asked. 'You know, at being a magician?'

'I failed the exam to get into magician school,' Gran said. 'Got caught out by the trick questions.'

I grinned, despite my mood. Gran's stupid jokes always cheered me up.

17

'Nothing happens overnight,' Gran said. 'Success takes time and hard work, and a good attitude. You have to keep rowing the boat. You have to get back on the horse. You have to pick yourself up and put that smile back on your face. You have to –'

'OK, OK, I get it.' I sighed again.

Then I heard the Bow Bells ringing half past eight and I realised I was going to be late for school. I dragged myself to my feet, kissed Gran's lavender-scented cheek, patted Lucky on the head and headed for the door.

2

The Best-Laid Plans

The good news was that it was the last
week of term before the summer holidays.
I was looking forward to weeks of doing
nothing but working on the stall, eating ice
creams and hanging around with my friends
Daisy, Sophie and Stretch. I also had a
plan for putting on a magic show in one of

the empty stalls at the market, to make a bit of money. The idea was foolproof – as long as we kept out of sight of PC Peaceful, the nosy local police officer.

I caught up with my friends at the school gates and told them about the plan. 'I can do tricks. Stretch, you can do your acrobatics thing with the teacups. Sophie, you can handle the money side of things. Daisy, you can do stunts.'

'Why do I get stuck with the money side of things?' Sophie asked with a frown.

'You can do a song and dance routine, if you'd prefer?' I suggested.

She shook her head. 'No thanks. On second thoughts, I'll stick to what I'm good at.' She took out her Business Book and started making notes.

'So, are you in?' I asked Stretch.

'Sure,' Stretch replied. 'I wanted to go to gymnastics camp, but Dad says we can't afford it.'

'Sorry, mate,' I said. 'It's rubbish having no money, isn't it?' Stretch's dad also has a market stall on Petticoat Lane, selling crockery. They're even tighter for money than we are.

'I told Dad to put it on a credit card,' he said. 'He said then we would **both** have an outstanding balance.'

'What about you, Sophie?' I said. 'You're always looking for a great business opportunity.'

'That's right, I am!' Sophie said as we walked into school. 'That's why I'm doing a Young Entrepreneurs' Course online next week.'

'A Young Entrepreneurs' Course.' I shuddered. 'I think I'd rather jump off a cliff.'

'Ooh,' Daisy chipped in. 'If we're jumping off a cliff, count me in.' There's a reason her nickname is Dangerous Daisy.

'Well, I'm looking forward to it,' Sophie said. 'It'll be nearly as good as school.'

'I don't understand how you can love school so much,' I said. 'Especially this school.'

Our school had a bit of a reputation, to be honest. Though Mr Singh said things were improving. We hadn't had a serious injury for nearly two months. Behaviour was always particularly bad in the last week

 23

before the holidays – it was like everyone had given up, including the teachers. A lot of people came in their own clothes instead of uniform: I saw three West Ham football kits, five Minecraft onesies and Athina from my class had come in wearing a T-Rex costume.

I kept my eye out for George Bottley, the class bully. We always gave him a wide berth, but sometimes he would sneak up on us when we were least expecting it.

'You said you were going to work harder at school,' Sophie said with a frown.

'I give 110% at school,' I said. '20% on Monday, 20% on Tuesday, 20% on Wednesday, 20% on Thursday and a big 30% push on Friday.'

We made our way to our lockers to put away our bags. Mr Singh was on corridor duty and looking harassed, as usual. He noticed us arrive and came over.

'Congratulations on yesterday, Max,' he said. 'I thought you were the best. And your assistant George Bottley, of course!'

'Oh yes,' I said. 'I was sorry to hear about George.'

He looked alarmed. 'Why, what happened to him?'

'Oh, nothing,' I replied. 'I'm just always sorry to hear about George. Looking forward to the holidays?'

'One more week,' he said with a wan

smile. 'We just have to get through one more week.'

Then his attention was caught by a shrieking student whizzing past on a pair of roller blades.

'Oi, stop skating in the corridor!' he yelled, heading off in pursuit. 'And put some trousers on!'

Just then, a shadow fell over us and I turned to see a huge figure approaching. A huge, unwelcome figure.

Bottley the Bully.

Everyone tensed. I narrowed my eyes. The last time I'd seen Bottley had been yesterday, at the final of The Greatest Show on Earth.

He had betrayed me and left me
dangling over the stage, ruining my act.
I'd got my revenge by casting a spell on
him.

Was **he** going to get his revenge now?
By pounding me to a pulp? Smashing me to
smithereens? Grinding me into gruel?

'Hi, Max,' he said. 'Can I carry your
bag?'

I looked at him suspiciously.

'What did you say?' I asked.

'Can I carry your bag?' he repeated. 'And yours, Daisy? Stretch? Have you had a haircut, Sophie? It suits you. Nice length.'

Everyone backed away a bit and we shook our heads.

'Oh, OK,' he said, undaunted. 'Do any of you need help with anything else? I'm not very good at homework, but I'm good at fixing bikes. Or fishing reels. I could take you fishing!'

'That's very kind of you, Bott– George,' I said. 'We'll let you know if we need your help with anything, OK?'

'Any time,' he said. 'Any. Time. Just let me know. All I want to do is help.'

'Did you do that?' Daisy asked, once he'd gone.

I nodded. The suggestion spell I'd cast on George Bottley was to make him more considerate and helpful.

'Are you just going to leave him like that?' Stretch asked.

I didn't know how to answer that. I was surprised to see that the spell hadn't worn off. I still had a lot to learn about my magical abilities, and it seemed that once I'd cast a spell on something, it stayed until it was removed.

'I feel kind of bad,' I said. 'But on the other hand, I definitely prefer helpful Bottley to Bottley the Bully.'

'He's kind of annoying,' Daisy said. 'But yeah, it's better than getting pounded by him.'

'Maybe he'll become a useful member of society,' Sophie said.

'Anything is possible,' I said.

After school I headed to the market on Petticoat Lane, as I always did. It was my job to cover for Dad on the toy stall for an hour or so while he went home for his tea. This was always my favourite time of the day.

'Dad,' I said, as he was grabbing his bag, preparing to go, 'Gran did this trick today where she went into an empty wardrobe, closed the door and came out a second later wearing a different dress.'

'Ah,' Dad said. 'The old Dress Switch trick. Classic. I once saw the great Barbara Cadabra do it at the Hackney Empire. Twelve complete dress changes in five minutes.'

'But how is it done?' I persisted.

'Easy,' Dad said. 'You wear one dress over the other. They're usually made out of silk so they're super-thin. If the stage lighting is down, people won't see that, or the little tabs you use to pull the dress off quickly, revealing the one underneath.'

I thought about this. The lights **had** been dim in the shop.

31

'But that means Gran must have planned it all in advance, just for me,' I said.

Dad smiled at me and ruffled my hair (which was already quite ruffled). 'Of course she did. I think she wanted to cheer you up.'

'She knew I was feeling down?' I asked, surprised.

Dad hunkered down so we were face to face. 'We all did, Max,' he said. 'We knew you'd be feeling flat after the contest. And you're not exactly great at hiding your emotions.'

'Well, you could have said something sooner,' I pointed out.

'Like what?'

'Like "Sorry you didn't win, Max. You

were robbed, Max. You were the best in our books, Max. Here's a bacon sandwich and a tenner, Max."'

'Ha!' he said. 'You did incredibly well. It would have been nice for you to win, but life goes on, Max. You have to pick up your feet and get walking. Now, let me show you these new toys that just came in. You should have a blast selling these.' He opened a big cardboard box behind the stall for me to look inside.

'Wow! Are those helicopters?' I asked.

'That's not the best bit,' Dad said. He pulled one out, took hold of a little handle on the side and twisted it half a dozen times.

 33

When he let go of the handle, the helicopter's blade spun with a whirring sound. Lights flashed on its tail and it lifted up from his hand and rose up into the air. Dad tapped it and the 'copter stopped, rotor spinning as it hovered in mid-air.

Then Dad blew on it and it began to fly in a slow circle, coming back to where it had started.

'**Unbelievable!**' I gasped.

'They stay hovering for a few minutes, then you have to wind them up again,' Dad said. 'I thought you could get a few of them in the air at a time to bring in the punters. Get them circling around your head, maybe.'

'I'll give it a spin,' I said with a cheeky smile.

'Hope you've got some better jokes,' he said. 'And try not to get a helicopter tangled in that mop you call a hairstyle.' He ruffled my hair again with a wink.

'Don't worry, Dad,' I said. 'I've got this. These will fly off the shelves.'

He groaned.

 35

Once Dad had gone, I started to set up. I was determined to sell as many of the little helicopters as I could.

So, here's the thing. When it comes to using my magic powers to 'help' me day to day, I have some rules. I don't like to cheat. I learned in the early days that misusing my powers tends to backfire. So I wouldn't use my magic to make the helicopters do anything the punters couldn't do when they got them home. That's not fair on the customer, and would just lead to a load of complaints. But I could use my powers to make the show a touch more . . . compelling. And it's all about the show, right?

Using my telekinesis, I wound up a dozen of the helicopters, then let them all go at once. Next, I summoned up a gentle breeze to get them all moving. That way, I could just let them do their thing, and concentrate on selling.

Summoning up the breeze brought back memories of the time I'd caused a much more mighty wind to sweep through the marketplace, upsetting the stalls and sending hundreds of banknotes flying into the air. The money had been stolen by a couple of local crooks, Barry and Gary Crayfish, who were now behind bars, thanks to me.

You're welcome.

My show soon attracted a gaggle of
punters. The nearby stall owners grinned
and nudged each other as they saw me hop
up onto the stall, with my trademark top hat
on my head at a jaunty angle.

'My uncle's a helicopter pilot,' I began. 'He says the job has its ups and downs.'

The old ones are the best. And the bad ones are the best too. A lady rolled her eyes at me, then followed it up with a grin.

'When he told me he was a fully qualified helicopter pilot, I said "Props to you."'

A ripple of laughter.

'He's not the brightest,' I went on. 'He had a crash the other week. The investigators asked him what happened, and he told them he got a bit cold and turned off the big fan on top.'

A bigger laugh, and a few groans.

'They took his licence, so he went to

39

work in a helicopter factory instead,' I went on. 'They didn't want him to get overworked, so they put him on a rota.'

A couple of young girls giggled and pointed at the helicopters. I saw their mum looking and nodding and smiling.

'Why do you often see a helicopter next to a hospital?' I asked a young man who'd stopped to watch.

He shrugged.

'Because it's too big to fit inside,' I said.

He laughed.

'I don't do a lot on social media,' I said, 'but last week I made a post about a helicopter and it really took off.'

'They're getting worse,' someone shouted.

'Show 'em to the doctor,' I called back.

I had a small crowd now. I couldn't make it too large, or PC Peaceful would be on my case for disturbing the peace, or obstructing the street, or having too much fun or something like that.

The helicopters were a massive success. Dad was absolutely over the moon when he got back after his tea. He gave me a ten-pound note as a thank-you and I headed off to Gran's to pick up Lucky with a skip in my step.

Even better, when I arrived, Gran had made some muffins. 'Just one, Max,' she said. 'Any more than that and you'll spoil your dinner.' Although that was complete

 41

nonsense, because I can eat an entire dinner before dinner without spoiling my dinner.

I left the shop feeling chirpy, but when I got home my good mood evaporated quickly.

There was a police car outside our house.

3

What's All This Then?

My first thought was that they'd come to arrest me. I wasn't sure what for, but I must have done something, surely?

Then I suddenly worried that someone had been hurt, or worse . . . Mum, or Dad? Not Gran, surely, because I'd just seen her. But one of my siblings?

I rushed inside and heard my mum call for me to go into the sitting room. I went in, my heart pounding, and saw my parents sitting on the sofa. Dad should have still been at the market, so whatever this was, it must be serious. Opposite them were two police officers – PC Peaceful and a plain-clothes officer who I didn't know.

'Max,' Mum said, 'I'm glad you're back – we were starting to get worried. You know PC Peaceful, don't you? And this is Detective Sergeant Vicky Young.'

'Is someone hurt?' I asked.

'No, no,' Mum said. 'Nothing like that.'

I breathed a sigh of relief. Then, 'Have you come to arrest me?' I asked nervously.

'What for?' PC Peaceful asked, eyes narrowed.

'Er, nothing, ha ha,' I said. 'Just my little joke.'

'Why don't you sit down?' the detective said.

Now that I knew no one had been hurt and it didn't seem I was immediately going to be arrested, I felt a lot happier. I sank down onto the sofa next to my mum.

'I want this to be a free conversation,' Vicky said in that way grown-ups do when they've done a course in 'talking

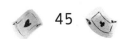 45

to children'. 'And I want you to tell me if there's anything you're uncomfortable with or anything that you don't like.'

'OK,' I said. 'I don't like your shoes.'

'Max!' Mum snapped.

'Sorry, just kidding.'

'It's OK,' Vicky said. 'I understand you're probably nervous.'

'Maybe it's time to actually say why you're here,' Dad prompted her.

'We're here to inform you that Barry and Gary Crayfish have escaped from prison,' the detective said.

My heart dropped into my boots. Suddenly I didn't feel quite so giddy.

'Now, I don't want you to be overly

concerned,' Vicky went on. 'They're not likely to come back to their old haunts. They will know we're looking for them, and they'll be easily recognised by just about everyone in the East End.'

I wasn't quite as sure as Detective Vicky. I knew how angry Barry Crayfish had been when I'd outsmarted him and scattered all his money across the market.

'But just to be on the safe side,' Detective Vicky went on, 'the City of London police force has arranged for you and your family to get away from London for a couple of weeks. We're confident that by then the Crayfish Twins will be safely back behind bars.'

'Where are you sending us?' I asked. I had visions of a safe house in some quiet corner of the country, like Northumbria, or a ramshackle farmhouse in the Welsh countryside. Or maybe they'd send us further afield – to Idaho or Tasmania.

'It's a flat in Acton,' the detective said.

'Acton?!' I exclaimed.

'It's in West London,' PC Peaceful
explained.

'I know where Acton is,' I said. 'I just
don't want to go there.'

'I'm sorry, Max,' Vicky said. 'We've
been asked to cut our budget for this sort
of thing. We used to send people to Bupkins
Leisure Park.'

'I want to go to Bupkins!' I said. 'I don't
want to go to smelly old Acton.'

'I'm sorry,' the detective said. 'Acton is
much cheaper than Bupkins.'

'You can't get a cheaper place then
Bupkins!' I protested.

'You clearly haven't been to Acton,' the
detective said.

Then I had an idea. A **magical** idea. I'd used the power of suggestion to make Bottley a better person. I could make people believe something, or say something, or do something, simply by suggesting it to them. I breathed in and felt the magic rise in my chest.

'I **suggest** you change your mind,' I said. 'I think you can find the money to send us all to Bupkins.'

'Max!' Mum said. 'Don't be so rude to the detective.'

'You know what?' Vicky said, a strange look on her face, as though she'd just had the most amazing idea. 'Actually, I **do** think it would be better for you to go to Bupkins.

It's further away from the East End, and hardly the sort of place the Crayfish Twins might turn up.'

Mum and Dad looked at each other in surprise.

'And my friends, too?' I asked. 'I **suggest** they might be in danger too and need to be kept safe.'

'Don't push it, Max!' Dad snapped.

Vicky nodded. 'Yes. I agree. You, your friends and your family should all go.'

'Excuse me?' Mum said. She and Dad looked totally flabbergasted.

I grinned evilly. 'All of us?'

'All of you,' Vicky replied.

'Even Gran?'

'Oh yes, we can get a ticket for her too.'

I tried not to cackle like a wicked crone. OK, so it wasn't Wales or Tasmania. But I had **always** wanted to go to Bupkins. Beach fun, activities, fish and chips, ice cream. And best of all, the entertainment. They had singing and dancing and comedy and . . . MAGIC! Gran and Grandad used to perform at Bupkins, back in the day. There were old photos of them onstage there, looking young and happy.

My mind immediately turned to how I could get myself up onto that stage. Maybe they did open-mic nights? This could be my chance to make up for losing The Greatest Show on Earth. I closed my eyes and imagined myself onstage at Bupkins, soaking up the applause. Breathing in the atmosphere.

This was going to be absolutely epic . . .

'One thing to remember,' Vicky said, 'is that you need to keep a **very** low profile. No getting yourself noticed.'

'No magic shows,' Mum said. 'You can leave your top hat at home. In fact, it'll be a good opportunity to catch up on your schoolwork. Get away from the stall and magic for a while, yes?'

'I **suggest** –' I began.

'MAX!' Mum snapped, glaring at me. 'Zip it!'

I looked around the room, shaking my

 53

head. Why were grown-ups like this? I'd
finally been offered the chance to get away
and have a proper holiday, with my friends,
but I wasn't going to be able to enjoy
myself.

I sighed. 'Fine,' I said. But it wasn't
fine. I wasn't going to let Max the
Magnificent miss out on this opportunity.
No way.

The next day when I woke up, all my negativity was gone. I was excited again, ready for the opportunities I knew were coming my way. I pointed at my top hat and it flipped off the dresser, straight onto my head. Then I did a little dance around the room while Lucky watched me, one eyebrow raised.

After the police officers had left the evening before, the whole family had sat down at the dinner table to talk things over.

'I'm not going,' Dad had said.

'Me neither,' Mum said.

'What?!' I cried. 'You have to come – we all have tickets. We never get to go away on holiday together.'

 55

'This is my busiest time of the year,' Dad said. 'London is full of tourists. I can't just pack up the stall for two weeks.'

'And things aren't great at work,' Mum said. 'It's not a good time to be leaving.'

'But won't you be in danger from the Crayfish Twins?' Susie asked.

Dad shook his head. 'The detective didn't seem to think so. It's Max and his friends they might be after. We've spoken to your friends' parents, and they are all happy for you to go as long as Chris, Vinny and Susie are there to provide adult supervision.'

'So this means Chris is in charge,' Mum said. 'You do what he says, OK?'

I looked at my older brother, who was currently tinkering with an old laptop, ignoring questions about what he was doing. Knowing my brother, it was highly unlikely that he would be attentive enough to actually do any active supervision of me or my friends.

'Fine,' I said. In fact, I could predict exactly what was going to happen. Chris would get involved in some electrical engineering task. Susie would spend all her time in the spa or on the beach. Vinny would find a football game to join and we would be left entirely to our own devices. Perfect.

'Gran's going to come though, right?' I asked. Of course Gran was going to come.

She wouldn't be able to resist returning to the scene of her past glories.

'I'm not sure,' Dad said. 'I called her last night and she said she'd think about it. Why don't you go and see her later and ask?'

'You mean on my way to school?' I asked.

'You're not going to school,' Mum said. 'The detective thought it was too risky.'

This was getting better and better!

I scoffed down my breakfast and pretty much ran to Gran's shop, weaving in and out of businesspeople, Spanish tourists and local residents who thronged the

pavement at this time of the morning.
Lucky grumbled along behind me,
complaining that he hadn't done his Puppy
Pilates yet and was feeling stiff.

'Gran is going to **love** the idea of
returning to Bupkins,' I said as we
reached the antique shop.

I pushed the door, but it was locked.
That was odd. Gran always opened early.
I had my own key, so I unlocked the door.

'Gran?' I called as I entered. But the
shop was empty.

Lucky rushed in and through to the back
room. I followed him, but Gran wasn't in
there either. Maybe she was still upstairs,
in the little flat above the shop where she

59

lived. I couldn't remember ever coming to the shop when Gran wasn't behind the counter, shuffling around among the stock, or in the back room baking brownies or oat cookies. Speaking of baking, the oven was on and I could smell something delicious. Gran must be around somewhere.

I was about to call up the stairs when Lucky cocked his head. 'Max,' he said, 'I can hear voices. From the basement.'

He trotted to the top of the stairs and stopped. He seemed unsure whether he should go down.

'Who could Gran be talking to down in the basement?' I asked. He shrugged. I moved past him, stepped onto the first step and went down, suddenly feeling nervous. My chest began to tingle with that familiar feeling I get when there's magic about.

Then I heard Gran speak.

'I think it's time,' she said.

And a voice answered her. A strange voice, thin and whispery, like from an old film. 'Time to go? Or time to tell him?'

'Both,' Gran said.

'Are you sure he's ready?'

'He'll have to be,' Gran said.

Lucky rushed past me at that point and barked, but when I reached the basement, Gran was alone.

She bent to scratch Lucky behind the

ears. When she straightened, I saw her face contract in pain.

'Is it your hips?' I asked, concerned.

'And the rest,' she said.

'Who were you talking to just now?' I asked.

Gran paused for a second, then said, 'No one, Max. Just talking to myself. It's the only way I can get some intelligent conversation around here.'

I thought about pressing her on it. I had definitely heard two voices. But if she didn't want to talk, then that was up to her. I had some secrets of my own, after all.

'Come on,' she said. 'Help me up these

steps – I need to open the shop. You can make me a cup of tea.'

As I helped her up, I thought I caught a flicker of movement out of the corner of my eye. I turned and looked back at the chest in the corner of the room. Was there something there?

'So, are you excited to be going back to Bupkins?' I said as I turned on the kettle.

'I'm not going,' she replied. 'I'm staying right here.'

I froze. Then I looked at her in astonishment. 'But you heard the news. The Crayfish Twins are on the loose. They might come here – they know who you are.'

'The Crayfish family has been around

here my whole life,' Gran says. 'I'm
not afraid. Besides, I'm not completely
defenceless.' She winked.

'I thought you'd jump at the chance
of going back to Bupkins,' I said. 'That's
where you got your big break. That's where
you first met Grandad.'

Gran turned and shuffled over to look
at a photo on the wall. It was her and
Grandad on a stage in sequinned outfits,
grinning from ear to ear. Grandad, who was
the spitting image of my dad, held a top
hat very similar to the one currently on my
head. Gran held a surprised-looking rabbit,
which she'd presumably just pulled out of
the hat.

'That's all in the past,' Gran said. 'It's time for a new star to shine in Suffolk. Time to hand over the stage.' She turned and grinned at me, her eyes twinkling.

Then the doorbell tinkled and Gran went to deal with the customer.

'Keep an eye on the brownies,' she said as she left. 'Don't let them burn.'

I went back to finish making the tea. But on my way, I saw the open door leading down to the basement, and I couldn't help myself.

'Max . . .' Lucky said, watching me.

I'm supposed to be the one who can read minds, but I think Lucky was even better at it than I was.

'I'll just be a second,' I said. I'm not sure what I was hoping to find down there. The owner of the mysterious voice? Maybe part of me felt that it was time to open the chest again. Time to get myself a new power. Something I could use at Bupkins to make a name for myself. To take over the stage, like Gran had said.

I got to the bottom of the steps, Lucky trotting along behind me, and crossed the floor to stand in front of the chest. A moment of doubt crossed my mind, then I reached out and took a firm hold of the lid.

'Don't do it, Max,' Lucky growled.

I stepped back, away from the chest.

'Thank goodness,' Lucky said.

I took off my top hat, grabbed a dented old soldier's helmet from a pile of old suitcases and put it on my head, pushing the chin strap into place. Then I stepped forward again.

'Oh, Max.' Lucky sighed. Then he dived under a table.

I opened the chest.

4

Stop the Clocks

FLASH!
BOOM!

I was thrown across the room.

 69

Of course I was getting used to it by now. I picked myself up and dusted myself off. The helmet had saved my bonce from a bash.

I looked around. Was something different? Did I have a new power?

Lucky peered out from behind the table leg suspiciously.

I shrugged. 'Nothing obvious,' I said.

Suddenly there was a piercing shriek. Lucky darted back to the safety of his table. I looked around frantically, expecting to be set upon by demon-ghouls from Planet X.

'Max!' Gran called from upstairs. 'The brownies are burning!'

When I got home, the house was utter
chaos – even more so than usual. We were
leaving for Bupkins the next day. Susie
had four huge suitcases filled with clothes,
make-up, swimming costumes and so on.
She had one suitcase entirely devoted to
hair products. Chris had filled his bag with
electronic items: circuit boards, electric
motors, computer parts and so on, as well
as various toolkits.

Whatever his secret project was, it would certainly keep him busy. He was currently trying to get the back wheel off an e-scooter as the whole scooter wouldn't fit in his case. Vinnie's bag was full of footballs, air pumps, boots, kit and football magazines.

'Aren't you taking any clothes?' Mum asked him.

He pointed to a West Ham shirt.

'Is that it?' Mum asked.

'Of course not,' he said. 'I'm also taking the away kit.'

I escaped up to my room to call my friends. Everyone was very excited about the holiday. And about the fact that we'd miss the last four days of school. Well, everyone except Sophie, who genuinely loved school.

'This is so cool!' Daisy said, her eyes bright. 'It's like we're going into Witness Protection!'

'It's not Witness Protection,' I said.

'Should we all change our names?' Stretch suggested. 'I want to be Jimmy Houston. No, Rudy Detroit. No, er, Malcolm Sacramento.'

'Will you wear a false moustache?' Daisy asked me. 'I will if you will.'

'Take it seriously, guys,' Sophie said. 'It must be a very worrying time for poor Max and his family. It's not "cool".'

'Actually, it **is** kind of cool,' I said.

'I definitely think it's cool,' Stretch said. 'What's cooler than being in mortal danger and on the run from a pair of crazed gangsters?'

'Are we in mortal danger?' Sophie asked.

'Hope so,' Daisy said, her eyes shining with excitement.

'I thought the Crayfish Twins were coming after you, Max,' Sophie pointed out. 'I'm not sure they even know who we are.'

'Do you want to come or not?' I asked.

'Yes, I do,' Sophie said, nodding furiously.

'They have Extreme Danger Sports there,' Daisy said. 'I checked the website. There's coasteering and rock climbing and white-water rafting and cliff jumping.'

'That sounds dangerous,' Sophie said.

'I know,' Daisy said, her eyes bright. 'There's only a slim chance that I'll make it back alive. It's going to be great!'

'Do they have tea at Bupkins?' Stretch asked.

'They have **free** tea,' I said. 'Twenty-four hours a day.'

'This is going to be amazing,' Stretch said.

Just then, I saw something move behind Stretch. 'What's that?' I asked.

Stretch turned. 'Oh, it's my MegaTed 9000,' he said, moving aside to give us a better view. The teddy bear was walking around the room. It picked up a T-shirt and folded it carefully before placing it in Stretch's chest of drawers.

'That bear is still going?' I asked. I had used my magic to animate this bear, along with fifty others, to sell at the market stall as part of our plan to pay off the Crayfish Twins. I was astonished that it was still going. I'd assumed the magic would wear off after a while.

'Um, yeah,' Stretch said, looking slightly embarrassed.

'Why didn't you tell us?' I asked.

'I didn't want you to know I had a teddy bear.'

'Is he tidying your room?' I asked.

'Yeah.' Stretch laughed nervously. 'He also does my homework.'

'Does he do it well?'

Stretch shrugged. 'Better than me, to be fair.'

'By the way,' I said, 'I opened the chest again.'

'MAX!' Sophie said.

'Did you get a new power?' Daisy asked. 'Fireballs?'

'I don't know,' I said. 'I don't feel any different. Maybe this time the genie decided not to grant me a new power. It's capacious, remember?'

'Capricious.' Sophie sighed. 'Just say "unpredictable" if you can't remember the word "capricious".'

'For all I know, maybe it's taken one of my powers away,' I said.

There was still quite a lot we didn't know about the genie. But we had found Arthur Andrews's diary, which detailed how he'd found the chest with the genie inside. It had granted Arthur the power of levitation. There didn't seem to be any rhyme or reason for what powers it granted, or to whom.

Just then there was a huge crash from downstairs, and the sound of shouting.

'I'd better go!' I said.

When I got downstairs, things were more chaotic than ever. Vinnie and Chris were

shouting angrily at each other. Lucky filled me in on what had happened. Chris had managed to get the back wheel off his e-scooter but about a million ball bearings had fallen out and scattered over the dining-room floor. Vinnie, doing keepy-uppies, had slipped on the ball bearings and crashed to the ground, giving the ball one last kick. The ball had flown through the door to the kitchen, knocking the chip pan over, which had caught alight. Dad was beating at the flames with a pair of pink oven gloves and yelling at Andrea, the cut-price smart-home device we have which for some reason only works if you speak to her in Spanish. He was currently trying to get Andrea to shut up.

'Silencio! **Silencio!**' he screamed.

Susie and Mum seemed oblivious to all that was going on. They were still arguing about whether Susie was allowed to take a fifth suitcase.

'I need it for my curlers,' she said.

'You already packed your hair curlers,' Mum pointed out.

'I mean my eyelash curlers!' Susie exclaimed.

After explaining the events to me, Lucky had rushed off and was now barking his head off, having the time of his life. No one but me could tell what he was saying,

 81

but it was, 'This is fun! This is fun! This is fun!' Sometimes dog barks aren't saying anything very interesting, to be honest.

I stood there shaking my head, my ears ringing. Suddenly it was all too much.

'**Stop!**' I screamed.

And do you know what?

They did stop. All of them. In fact, **everything** stopped.

Chris and Vinnie stopped yelling. Mum and Susie stopped arguing. Dad stopped beating the flames.

The flames stopped flickering.

Lucky stopped barking.

There was no noise. None at all. Even the clock on the wall had stopped ticking.

I looked over at it. It hadn't just stopped ticking. The second hand wasn't moving.

The clock had stopped altogether.

Time itself had stopped.

'Oh no,' I muttered.

5

Nope

So now I knew what my new power was.
Being able to freeze time.

I walked up to Dad, nearly slipping
over on the ball bearings, and poked him.
He swayed slightly, but didn't wake up.
He just stood staring at the flaming pan.
I looked at the pan and moved my hand

 85

closer to the flames. There was no heat. The flames weren't even flickering. Then I had a thought. I went to the cupboard where Mum and Dad kept all the instruction books for the kitchen appliances. I flicked through the user guide for the stove and found what I was looking for. 'What to do in the event of an oil fire': put the pan lid or a baking sheet over the pan to starve it of oxygen. Shut off the heat and don't move the pan or remove the lid until it has cooled completely.

'Fair enough,' I said to myself. I found the lid, covered the pan and switched off the gas burner beneath it.

Then I took out the dustpan and brush and swept up the ball bearings.

Finally, I turned Andrea off at the wall.

Now that the emergency things were dealt with, I had no choice but to stop and think about the situation.

This was big. Really big. All my magical powers were pretty scary, when you thought about it. The ability to move things by thought alone. The ability to make terrifying illusions, the ability to read minds and the power to make people do things they didn't want to do. All of them had got me into trouble. I had to be careful about when I used them, and **why**.

But this was something else. The ability to stop time altogether? My heart pounded at the possibilities. I could walk into any

bank in the world and steal all the money.
I could win the 100 metres at the Olympic
Games. I could get to the front of the queue
in the school canteen!

I didn't like it. I didn't like it one bit.
What was the genie trying to do to me? Test
me? Trick me into doing something stupid?
To be honest, if you want me to do something
stupid, you don't need to trick me into it.
You just have to wait. So why?

But that was a question for another time.
There was a bigger question facing me right
now. How was I going to **start** time again?
I didn't fancy living here on my own for the
rest of my life. And what if time had stopped
for me too? What if I never grew old? What

if I was stuck at this age for ever?! I'd never grow a moustache, I'd never finish school, I'd never be able to get into a 12A movie on my own. I shivered at the thought.

The silence was terrifying too. There's always **some** noise. I'd never ever in my life experienced complete, utter, dead silence like this. I cleared my throat. The noise sounded flat.

'S-start?' I said. Nothing happened.

'Begin?' I tried. Nothing.

I thought for a while. Then it came to me.

I shut my eyes. 'GO!' I yelled.

Blessed, wonderful noise filled the room, assaulting my ears.

'Look at all these ball bearings!' Vinnie yelled. Then he looked down, saw the clean floor and frowned.

'ANDREA, SILENCIO!' Dad yelled. Then, noticing that Andrea was already quiet, he looked to the chip pan and blinked in surprise to see the lid and no flames.

Mum and Susie resumed their argument as though nothing had happened. Which, I suppose, for them nothing had.

Lucky stopped barking, as though **he'd** noticed something had changed. He looked at me and I nodded at him. Something had changed.

Everything had changed.

'Just think of what you could do with this power!' Lucky pleaded.

'Don't care,' I said. 'I'm not using it.'

'You could freeze time, travel to scenes of disasters and save people,' he said. 'You could climb Mount Everest. You could

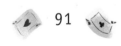

91

sneak into the bacon factory and steal all the world's bacon and become a bacon billionaire.'

'It's too much,' I said. 'Too dangerous. What if I break something? What if I destroy something? What if the power goes to my head? Remember when I made that massive worm come out of Bottley's pocket?'

'There's a reason the genie gave you your powers, Max,' Lucky said. 'At some point you're going to have to figure out what that reason is. You'll need to use your powers for something big. Something important. Probably something to do with bacon.'

'I don't know,' I said. 'This feels bigger than bacon.'

'Nothing is bigger than bacon,' Lucky said, deadly serious.

'How will the universe like it if I go around stopping time?' I asked him. 'What happens to all the suns and planets and black holes out there? Do they stop too? Does that cause any issues at . . . I don't know, the quantum level? Will Albert Einstein phone me up and shout at me? I don't want to destroy the entire universe just to get my family to stop talking for five seconds.'

The other thing I'd noticed was that since using the time-stop power I was

really tired. Using any of my magical abilities could be quite tiring, but this was something else. It felt as if I'd been swimming against a massive tide, fighting against the power of the universe itself. I ended up going to bed early, which everyone was astonished at, and I slept in too, but it didn't matter as I wasn't going to school!

Or so I thought.

'Sorry, Max,' Mum said when I came downstairs. 'You're going to need to put your school uniform on. You have to go in today.'

'What?!' I said. 'Why?!'

'Some of the other parents reminded

me this morning that you have a maths test today. You can come home early though. I'll give you a note.'

'Why is there a maths test in the last week of school?!' I cried.

'Better than it being in the first week of school,' Mum pointed out.

'No, it's not,' I replied crossly. 'Then we'd get it out of the way.'

'But you wouldn't have had time to learn anything!' Mum snapped.

'That's true,' I said. 'But on the other hand, I wouldn't have had time to forget anything either!'

'You're going in!' Mum snapped.

'But it's dangerous!' I said. 'The

Crayfish Twins might get me.'

'You'll be fine for one morning.' Mum sighed. 'Honestly, if you're hanging around the house all day, I might murder you myself.'

Life is a roller coaster, isn't it? One day you're having the time of your life, no school, about to head off to Bupkins with your best friends and your dog, not a care in the world. The next you're coming to terms with the fact that you have the magical ability to stop time and potentially destroy the universe – and even worse, you have a maths test.

By the time I'd changed into my uniform and left the house, I was running late. I usually left home when I heard the Bow Bells chime eight o'clock. They say if you are born within the sound of the Bow Bells, you are a true Cockney. Well, that's me. Unfortunately I didn't hear the bells that morning, so I was going to be late for school. I talked Mum into taking Lucky over to Gran's, which would save me a few minutes. But it wasn't going to be enough!

On the one hand, it didn't really matter, because it was the final week and no one really cared. Even most of the teachers had stopped caring.

On the other hand – Mr Hughes, the maths teacher. Mr Hughes was the most boring teacher in the whole school. And

it was a crowded field, let me tell you.
His voice was boring, his clothes were
boring, his face was boring. And of course
he taught the most boring subject of all.
Maths.

My big mistake had been to tell him how
boring maths was when he'd asked me why I
looked so glum one day. They tell you that
adults appreciate it when you are honest
with them.

Turns out that's not true.

Anyway, ever since then Mr Hughes
had been itching to give me a detention.
I really didn't want a detention. Because
that would mean I couldn't leave early, as
Mum had promised.

I groaned as I rushed along Cobb Street. Then I saw the number 56 bus. If I managed to catch it, I had a chance of getting to school on time. I ran for the bus and I thought I was going to make it – but then a large group of Spanish tourists came out of a shop and blocked the pavement.

'Permiso, **Permiso!**' I panted, darting through the group.

A couple of seconds before I made it to the bus stop, the driver pulled away.

My frustration boiled over and without thinking, I yelled, **'Stop!'**

The bus stopped.

And so did everything else. My determination not to use my new power

had lasted about twelve hours. I stood and turned around slowly. There was the woman who'd just got off the bus, paused mid-stride. There were the tourists blocking the pavement. There was a pigeon in mid-flight. There was a cycle courier running a red light, frozen in time.

I walked the few steps to the bus and hopped on. I took a seat, took a breath, then said, 'Go!'

I ran into Sophie outside maths.

'Have you studied for the test?' she asked brightly.

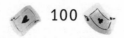 100

'No,' I replied. 'I'd forgotten it was happening.'

'Oh, Max.' She sighed.

'It's the last week of school!' I protested. 'How can there be a test in the last week of school?'

'Better than a test in the first week of school!' she said with a wink. I glared at her.

Half an hour later I found myself staring at a sheet of paper with weird squiggles on it. None of it made any sense. I find reading a real challenge at the best of times. I don't know why, but letters and words just don't sit still on the page for me. It takes me ages to

101

work out what a word says, let alone figure
out the answer to the question. And when
you throw in little symbols like divisions
or multiplications or square roots, it might
as well be Ancient Greek. Why couldn't
the genie have given me the power to read
properly?

Everyone else was scribbling away. I could
hear their pencils scratching across paper.
Mr Hughes walked up and down the aisles
with his boring walk, watching us all intently.

The funny thing is, I don't think I'm that
bad at maths, or English, or history. I just
struggle with reading the information. I need
more time, I thought, as I looked up at the
clock.

Time.

The second hand moved on. The minute hand juddered forward.

My heart beat faster.

Could I? Should I? Was it cheating? Surely, if all I was doing was giving myself more time to complete the questions, that wasn't cheating. It wasn't as if I was going to look up the answers.

I was just . . . rebalancing an unfair universe.

Maybe the universe **wanted** me to stop time, I thought.

I hesitated. I paused, I considered . . .

'Ten minutes to go,' Mr Hughes called. And that did it.

'**Stop**,' I said firmly.

And time stopped. I licked my pencil and got to work.

6

School's Out!

A day later, we were on a train heading towards Bupkins. We didn't get away from London very often, and it's possible that we might have been a little over-excited. Everyone had brought sweets and fizzy drinks, and we probably consumed more sugar in the first fifteen minutes of the

trip than is strictly advisable. People kept glaring at us. After ten minutes, Chris, Vinnie and Susie moved into a different carriage, pretending they didn't know us.

Stretch was doing flips in the corridor, Daisy was swinging from the arm rests, I was performing magic tricks for some children in a nearby bank of seats.

'You're Max Magic!' one of the mums said, as I pulled some scarves out of my sleeve.

I handed her a flower plucked from my other sleeve. 'Guilty as charged,' I said with a cheeky wink.

'We saw your show in Blackpool,' another mum told me.

'Sorry, no refunds,' I said with a smile.

Only Sophie was calm. 'Didn't the detective tell you not to draw attention to yourself?' she asked from behind me.

'What can I say?' I replied. 'My public love me, and I love them.'

The train journey seemed to take ages, but it must have felt like much longer to the poor people who were sharing a carriage with us.

The train station was just a few minutes' walk from Bupkins. We went straight to reception. Standing in the doorway was a massive model of Monty the Mongoose, the mascot of Bupkins. He was in all the TV ads and his picture was on all the cups

107

and napkins in the restaurants and cafes. Everyone loves Monty the Mongoose!

While Chris and Susie checked in, Vinny sat and read yet another magazine about West Ham and the rest of us hopped up and down excitedly, took selfies with Monty and generally were far too loud.

Can you tell we were excited?

As soon as Chris had the keys, I said, 'Great! Come on, guys, let's go and explore!'

'No!' Susie snapped. 'Let's take our bags to our cabins first.'

I sighed. All I wanted was to explore the park, but we dragged our bags to the accommodation area and found our cabins, which were actually quite sweet. I was sharing with Stretch. Daisy and Sophie were sharing the one next door.

'OK, let's dump our bags and meet back out here in thirty seconds,' I told them.

'Erm, aren't you going to unpack?'

Sophie said, staring at me as if I was mad.

'What for?' I asked.

'Unpacking is the best bit of the holiday,' Sophie said. 'Finding drawers for all your things, hanging your dresses up. Taking all your bathroom things out and arranging them on the shelf.'

I shook my head. 'It's like you and I are from two different species.'

'I wouldn't mind a cup of tea,' Stretch said.

'And I need to do my ju-jitsu exercises,' Daisy added. 'I lose my form if I don't practise every day.'

'We'll meet back here in half an hour,' Sophie said.

I gritted my teeth in frustration, but nodded.

I did not unpack my case. I didn't even open it. The way I saw it, I could do that when I needed something from it. Stretch did unpack his case – sort of. I lay on the bed trying to focus on a comic, but I could hear shouts and laughter echoing round the park. Everyone seemed to be having a great time and I was missing out because Sophie wanted to line up her toothpaste and toothbrush.

Then suddenly Stretch cried out, 'No!'

Lucky barked in alarm. I watched Stretch sink to the floor on his knees, shaking his head and saying, 'No, no, no,' again and again.

 111

'What is it?' I asked, springing to my feet and rushing over. 'Are you ill? Did you get bad news?'

'I forgot to pack my teapot,' he sobbed.

'What?!' I asked. 'They have a kettle in the room, with teabags and everything.' I pointed.

'It's not the same!' he cried.

'Don't worry, man,' I said. 'We'll find you a new teapot.'

'Thanks, Max,' he said, snuffling.

The comic wasn't really holding my interest, so I decided to practise the new card trick I'd been working on: Forcing a Card, which means making sure the person you are tricking takes the card you want them to.*

After what seemed like forever, we finally met up and spent the next hour racing around the resort, exploring and planning what we were going to get up to over the next couple of weeks.

There was a swimming pool complex with water slides. There was a funfair with rides that you could go on as many times as you liked – all for free. There were snack food cabins and a big mall building with entertainment and a food court. There was

* Turn to the back of the book to learn this trick!

a person dressed as Monty the Mongoose walking around waving and giving hugs to kids. But the thing I was most excited to see was the massive theatre at the far end of the park, with posters advertising the brilliant acts that would be performing there over the next few weeks: singers, dancers, comedians and, of course, magicians.

'Ooh,' Sophie said. 'They have bingo. I love bingo.'

'Hey, look at this, Max,' Daisy said, pointing to one of the posters.

The poster read:

OPEN-MIC NIGHT THIS THURSDAY

**ALL WELCOME.
REGISTER AT RECEPTION.**

'Yes, please,' I said.

 115

'No, thanks,' a voice said from behind me. I spun around to see who it was. It took me a moment to recognise him. I'd never seen him without his police uniform.

'**PC Peaceful!**' I gasped. 'What are you doing here?'

'Shh!' he said, looking around anxiously. 'I'm undercover.' He was wearing a Hawaiian shirt and sunglasses, even though the day was quite cloudy and cool.

'Why?' I asked.

'I'm here on a top-secret mission,' he said. 'There are two parts. One is to keep an eye on you kids and make sure you don't get into trouble.'

I groaned. Getting into trouble was the main point of existing, as far as I was concerned.

'The second is to keep an eye out for the Crayfish Twins and arrest them.'

'But why did they choose you?' I asked. 'Why not a real detective?'

PC Peaceful bristled. 'I'll have you know I took my detective exam again just yesterday.'

 117

'How many times have you taken it?' Sophie asked.

'Twelve,' he said proudly.

'Did you pass?' I asked.

'Just.'

'Good for you,' I said. And I meant it. I knew how hard it was to pass exams.

'So from now on,' he said, beaming proudly, 'you should address me as Detective Constable Peaceful, not PC Peaceful.'

'It doesn't trip off the tongue as well,' I pointed out.

He ignored that. 'Also,' he went on, 'I know the targets of the investigation well. I can easily recognise them, even if they are in disguise.'

'But they know you as well,' Daisy pointed out. 'If they see you, they'll know who you are. Even if you're in civilian clothes.'

'That's a good point,' DC Peaceful said, his face falling. 'I hadn't thought of that.'

'Maybe you need to wear a disguise,' I suggested.

'Like what?'

I shrugged. 'You'll figure it out.'

'Anyway,' DC Peaceful said, 'you need to keep a low profile. So definitely no open-mic night for you!'

I nodded. But there was no way I was going to do what Simon Peaceful told me, PC or DC. I'm Max the Magnificent!

 119

If he thought I was going to pass up an opportunity to be the star of the show at Bupkins, then he had another thing coming.

7

Kite Karma

I loved **everything** about Bupkins.

On the first morning, we decided to go to the beach. Susie was going to spend the day in the spa. Vinny had joined a five-a-side league and was going to play football all day. Chris agreed to be our minder for the day, and said he was going to use his

 121

home-made metal detector on the beach.

To be honest, the weather wasn't that great. It was a little showery, a little cold, and very windy. Susie was moaning that she wasn't going to get a suntan, but we didn't care. Lucky was in his element. He raced up and down the beach, little puffs of dust exploding under his paws as he skipped across the sand. It was as though the sea air had given him a new lease of life.

Our first stop was a beach shack called Aladdin's Cave. Stretch bought a bucket and spade. Daisy bought an inflatable boat. Sophie bought a sunshade and a new notebook.

And me? I bought a kite.

'Dad used to work in a kite factory,' I told the others as I was setting it up. 'He had to pull a few strings to get the job. Do you want to help me fly it?' I asked Stretch.

'No, thanks,' he said. 'I'm going to build the world's greatest sandcastle.'

It was perfect kite-flying weather. Lots of space to run, and lots of wind. As I walked proudly down to the firmer sand nearer the water, I could feel the kite pulling away, tugged upwards by the wind. This was going to be epic, I told myself. I lifted the kite high, ran twenty steps along the beach and let out some string.

The kite dived headfirst into the sand.

Hmm, I thought. No worries. Probably just caught a random downdraught.

I tried again. This time I ran thirty steps before letting go. I let out more string and yanked hard.

The kite spun around in a tight circle

three times before again rocketing down
into the sand, burying itself.

'Great kite,' Stretch yelled from where
he was building his sandcastle. Which was
already quite elaborate, with towers and
gardens and a moat.

I growled in annoyance and tried a
third time. This time I ran **forty** steps, by
which point I was really quite puffed. I
launched the kite high into the air, like a

 125

javelin thrower, and let out loads of string as quickly as I could.

The kite shot up!

I laughed triumphantly.

But then the kite flipped and dived, plunging even deeper into the sand this time.

I lost my temper and felt the familiar tingle in my chest as the magic inside me decided it was time to get involved. And I didn't suppress it, as I'd learned to do. I held out a finger and a little jolt of electricity tingled right down to the tip. The kite pinged up, out of the sand, and stayed there, quivering in the breeze.

I can't spell telekinesis. But I know how to do it.

I flicked my finger and the kite soared majestically into the air – up, up and up again. I played out the string, grinning wildly. I didn't care that I was cheating a little . . . well, a lot. It was just glorious to see the kite doing what it was supposed to. Doing what I wanted it to.

And what I wanted it to do was to hurtle down, skim across the sand and totally obliterate Stretch's sandcastle.

DOOSH!

'OI!' Stretch squawked through a mouthful of sand.

'**Sorry**!' I yelled. 'The kite's very hard to control.' I cackled evilly to myself. But then a massive gust of wind came along and yanked the kite string right out of my hands!

'No!' I cried as the kite went sailing off into the clouds, higher and higher until I couldn't see it at all.

'Don't worry, Max,' Lucky barked. 'I'll get it.' He raced off down the beach, but it was no use. The kite was lost.

Stretch walked over to me. 'That's called karma,' he said.

That afternoon, it rained. It rained so hard that even we were driven indoors while we waited for it to stop. Daisy went to the indoor climbing wall. Sophie went off to play bingo.

I was so bored that I agreed to a game of Scrabble with Stretch. Lucky was helping me, though of course Stretch didn't know that. He thought Lucky was just barking or whining.

That was until Lucky suggested I put down M-I-C-R-O-B-E on a triple word score.

Stretch narrowed his eyes suspiciously. 'Is Lucky helping you?' he asked.

'No!' I said, looking puzzled at the suggestion. 'He's just a dumb dog.'

 129

'Watch it, Max,' Lucky growled.

'OK, so what's a microbe?' Stretch asked.

'Er, a tiny dressing gown?' I suggested.

'Is it?' Stretch said. 'Oh, OK then.'

We got bored soon after that and decided to brave the rain and head down to the mall to see what was going on.

Chris had told us we were to stick together, but he, as expected, was in his cabin with an electric motor and a soldering iron. Vinny was off playing football, and as far as I knew, Susie was still in the spa under a sunbed. She was going to be as tanned as an orange that had just got back from a two-week holiday in Spain.

When we got to the mall, we wandered up and down for a while. There were loads of food places. Stretch was very excited by the look of the Monster Mongoose burger at Monty's Burger Shack. There was a little funfair too, with a roller coaster that ran around the mall, going overhead and up and around the high ceiling. There were a couple of big stages, with a dancercise class taking place on one and a puppet show on the other.

We found ourselves standing outside an attraction called the House of Horrors. Little kids were going in one door looking nervous and coming out the exit looking terrified. A sign over the entrance read:

131

PREPARE TO FACE YOUR GREATEST FEAR

'Maybe it's a maths test,' Stretch
suggested, nudging me.

I shuddered.

Then we found ourselves at the doors
to the big hall, where they have the special
shows with comedians and magicians and
pop groups. Today, though, the tables and
chairs had been cleared away and there
was a group from the World Dominoes
Corporation filming a documentary about
their attempt to break the world record

for the longest domino chain in a holiday resort in Suffolk. They were letting everyone help. The domino people were quite sensible and they made sure to put gaps between dominoes every so often so that the whole display wouldn't get knocked down if one of the kids accidentally kicked over part of it, which happened every five seconds or so.

I considered using my telekinesis to help set up the dominoes. But that would be cheating. There's no point in playing any game, or getting involved in anything, if you're just going to cheat your way through it. Stretch had been right earlier. Losing the kite had been payback for me

 133

knocking over his sandcastle, which had been a mean thing to do.

If I misused my powers, bad things happened.

Sophie appeared and started placing dominoes carefully and slowly.

'Max,' she said, 'do you really think you should be here?'

'Why not?'

She nodded towards one of the cameras. 'We're being filmed. What if the Crayfish Twins see you on the television?'

'I doubt Barry and Gary Crayfish are going to be watching a domino documentary on UKTV Kids Gold 4,' I pointed out.

'I just think you can't be too careful,'

she said, and set down another domino, very neatly. She was good at this, of course. Sophie is good at everything.

And maybe she had a point. I thought for a second, then grinned. 'I have an idea,' I said.

I closed my eyes, breathed deeply, and summoned my illusion power, imagining my face looking very different. I looked over at Sophie and said, 'Psst.'

She turned . . . and shrieked, leaping backwards and knocking over her own dominoes.

'Pretty good, huh?' I said.

'You look exactly like George Bottley!' she said. 'I hate it.'

 135

'Well, no one is going to recognise me now,' I said. I enjoyed using my illusion power, and this time I had a good excuse. This wasn't cheating. Just . . . helping.

Lucky knocked over my dominoes again, and I sighed and started over.

Setting up dominoes can be extremely time-consuming. Which I suppose is why the Bupkins people arranged it in the first place. What better way to keep fifty children quiet on a rainy afternoon while their parents had a snooze or went down the pub, or had a snooze in the pub?

Finally it was time to set off the main display. To do this, the organisers had to join up all the separated sections of dominoes. They asked all the children to stand well back to make sure no one set it off by accident! Lucky was more excited than anyone, and strained to get loose, but I held his leash tight. A voice crackled through the PA and began the countdown, with everyone in the crowd joining in. The cameras were poised at a dozen locations, ready to capture the big moment and follow the dominoes on their clever path.

'Four . . . three . . . two . . .'

Just then the double doors at the far end of the theatre banged open in the wind and something flew in. Children shrieked as something huge sailed over their heads, showering them with rain. Everyone turned

137

to look, and I knew instantly what it was.

'The **kite!**' Lucky shrieked as it sailed over his head. '**Max, it's your kite!**' He lunged and sprinted after it, snapping his jaws at the trailing string, just missing it. He ran so hard his leash pinged out of my hand. I cried out as I watched **my** dog chase **my** kite right through the middle of the world-record-breaking domino display, sending thousands of little black tiles flying.

Children were screaming, the organisers were shouting, Lucky was barking.

Twelve cameras followed the trail of destruction as Lucky chased after the kite.

The kite, which was clearly still filled with the telekinetic energy I'd given it on the beach, performed a beautiful somersault, then came back, passing over an as yet untouched part of the display. Lucky ploughed through that as well, barking joyfully. He followed the kite all the way back down the aisle, through the double doors and out into the howling wind. The doors slammed shut behind them.

For a moment, everything was deathly quiet.

I turned, my heart in my boots, to see twelve cameras, four domino crew members and fifty children all looking at me.

'Was that your dog?' one of the crew asked coldly.

'Um . . . yes,' I said.

'What's your name?' the young lady asked.

I felt the cameras zoom in on my face.

'George Bottley,' I said.

8

Suit Surprise

It was only after it was all over that I
wondered if that might have been a good
time to use my time-stop power. I could
have stopped time, then gone in and
retrieved Lucky and that pesky kite. Then
stopped the domino trail before they all
fell over.

Oh well, it was too late now. I could stop time, but I couldn't go back in time. Now **that** would be a scary power to have.

The next day, we all met up for breakfast. I'd ended the illusion and was glad to have my own devilishly handsome, cheeky but kind face back.

It seemed that Chris, Vinnie and Susie had basically given up on the idea of keeping an eye on us.

'How much trouble can you get into at a holiday resort anyway?' Chris had said, showing an extraordinary lack of imagination.

I did spot DC Peaceful sitting a few tables away, wearing socks and sandals

and a brightly coloured T-shirt. He nodded
at me quickly then looked away, pretending
not to know me. With him around, we
probably did have to be careful.

'What shall we do today?' Daisy asked.
'I feel like doing something dangerous.
Maybe the water flumes?'

'They don't seem very dangerous,'
Sophie pointed out.

'They are if you go down backwards and
upside down and wearing a blindfold,' Daisy
said. She looked thoughtful. 'I wonder if
you could fit a bike down one.'

Stretch was drinking his third cup of
tea. 'I think I might check out the climbing
wall,' he said.

'I'm going to play bingo,' Sophie said primly.

'Again?' Daisy asked.

'I have a system,' Sophie said with a sly smile. 'I think I can break the house and take them for everything they have.'

'The prizes are stuffed toys, sweets and pens,' I said. 'It's not exactly Las Vegas.'

'It's not about the prizes,' Sophie said. 'It's about the challenge. I'll meet up with you later.'

'What about you, Max?' Daisy asked. 'Wanna come to the water flumes with me?'

I shook my head. I had another plan.

'I hope you're not going to sign up

for the open mic,' Sophie said, eyeing me carefully.

I couldn't help glancing over at DC Peaceful.

'I'm not going to, no,' I said.

But George Bottley would, I thought, unable to stop a wicked grin from appearing on my face.

After breakfast I popped back to the cabin as Stretch headed off to the climbing wall. There was something I needed to try.

I opened my suitcase and pulled out the item I'd ordered off the internet

from Ronnie McMahon's Magic Zone, using a voucher Susie had bought me for my birthday. I unrolled it. It was a suit, bright green and made of very thin nylon. I hadn't been able to afford the silk version, of course, but the nylon would be fine as long as I stayed away from naked flames. Some of the reviews on Ronnie's website had been quite horrific to read.

I had decided to go with the Dress Switch trick (though in my case it was a Suit Switch), despite the danger of combustion, as it was cheap and simple. Surely the Bupkins people could find a wardrobe for the stage? I had toyed with the idea of performing the Mongolian Rope Trick, but apart from the difficulty involved in acquiring a pony, 10 metres of rope and a crossbow, the trick had recently been banned by the Magic Circle because of the danger it posed to the audience, the performer, and cultural relations between Britain and Mongolia.

I put the suit on over my shorts and T-shirt. It actually looked OK. Very garish, but that was what I wanted. It would certainly draw the eye onstage.

Then I took out the second item I'd bought. It was another suit. This one was bright red. I put that one on too. The fabric of each suit was so thin it was as if I was wearing nothing. The red suit completely covered the green one.

'OK, Lucky,' I said. 'Watch me.'

Lucky was asleep. I nudged him and he opened one eye and gave me an annoyed look. 'What on earth are you wearing?' he asked. 'I've seen some cheap suits in my time, but this takes the biscuit.'

'Never mind that,' I said. 'Just watch what I do now.' I opened the wardrobe door, stepped in and closed the door behind me. The red suit had little quick-release tabs on one side. One for the trousers, one for the jacket. I pulled them and the suit came away, revealing the green one underneath. I dropped the pieces of red cloth on the wardrobe floor and opened the door again.

'*DOOSH!*' I cried, stepping out. Unfortunately my foot got caught in the fabric of the red suit and I tripped, falling flat on the floor.

'Excellent stuff,' Lucky said sarcastically. 'If only I had the ability to clap.'

'OK,' I said, 'But apart from the trip, what do you think about the trick?'

'What trick?' Lucky asked.

I stared at him, incredulous. 'The change of clothes?! I just changed suits in three seconds.'

Lucky stared back at me, looking me up and down. 'No, you didn't,' he said. 'You were wearing a cheap suit when you went

 151

in and you're wearing the same cheap suit now.'

'I am **not**!' I said. 'The first suit was red. Does this look like red to you?!'

'I don't know what red is!' Lucky shouted back. 'Dogs are **colour-blind**!'

'Ah,' I said, the wind taken out of my kite. 'That is a good point. You're probably not the ideal audience for this trick.'

'You want to do magic tricks?' the open-mic organiser said with a frown. His name was Dan and he was wearing a green

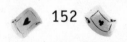

jacket, almost the same colour as my quick-change suit. 'Like card tricks?'

'Sure,' I said. 'But also, could I have a wardrobe?'

'You want me to bring a wardrobe out onto the stage during an open-mic event?' he asked.

'Is that a problem?'

'This isn't The Greatest Show on Earth,' he said. 'It's twenty kids telling bad jokes and doing dances they've learned on TikTok.'

'You're wrong,' I said. I turned and gestured at the stage. 'This is a theatre of dreams. This is where the magic starts. Glittering careers begin in places like this.

 153

Who knows what the kids of today will go on to achieve, if you only give them a chance now?'

The man sighed and looked at me like he wanted to wring my neck. Would I have to use my power of suggestion?

'Just one wardrobe,' I said with my most winning grin.

'Fine!' he snapped, and made a note on his clipboard.

Sometimes the best magic is just a smile.

I headed back to the cabin to get my swimming trunks. I was going to go to the

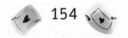

water park to meet up with Daisy. I had convinced Chris to take Lucky for a walk along the beach, as dogs were definitely not welcome in the water park. Nor were bikes, as one of the staff had had to explain to Daisy earlier.

'Psst!' a voice said. I spun and looked around, but I couldn't see anyone I recognised. Just a poor person in a Monty the Mongoose outfit.

'Psst!' the mongoose said. 'It is I, PC Peaceful. I mean, DC Peaceful.'

I walked over and peered into the mongoose's mouth, to see DC Peaceful. 'What are you doing in a mongoose?' I asked.

 155

'Disguise,' he hissed, then looked up and
down the concourse. 'Keeping an eye out
for the Crayfish Twins.'

'Oh,' I said. 'Excellent. Well, keep up
the good work. If you want someone to
arrest, I think I saw some squirrels stealing
nuts in the cafe earlier.' I winked and
turned to go.

'Wait,' he said. 'Did I just see

you coming out of the theatre? You're
not thinking of entering the open-mic
competition, are you?'

'Definitely not,' I said, looking
offended. 'You certainly won't see Max
Magic onstage tomorrow night.'

He narrowed his eyes and looked at me.
'OK, well, I'd better not, is all I can say. I
will be attending, just so you know.'

'In the mongoose outfit?'

'No, I have something else to wear
tomorrow night,' he said frostily.

'Me too,' I said. 'See you later, DC
Mongoose.'

 157

I stood in the wings, feeling really quite nervous. Compared to The Greatest Show on Earth, this audience was tiny. And mostly it was made up of the mums and dads of the kids in the show. The organiser had been right of course: most of the acts were terrible. No one had practised anything and the jokes were awful. But everyone seemed to be having a good time.

And I'd meant what I'd said yesterday to Greenjacket Dan. Every performance was important, no matter how many people were watching. A great performer had to put on a great show every time. Gran had been right: after losing The Greatest Show on Earth, the only thing to do was pick myself up and start again. And here I was.

Or, to be more accurate, here was George Bottley. I'd changed my face again, using my illusion power. Every time I looked in the mirror, I terrified myself, thinking Bottley had appeared to squash me against a wall like a bug.

The previous act had just finished and had received a smattering of applause. I was pleased to see Greenjacket Dan hadn't forgotten the wardrobe; a stagehand wheeled it onto the stage on a little trolley and left it right in the middle.

'And now we have a real treat for you,' Greenjacket Dan shouted into the

 159

microphone. 'We have a magician! Ladies and gentlemen, boys and girls, it is my great pleasure to introduce to you . . . Bottley the BRILLIANT!'

The first and last time anyone would refer to Bottley as brilliant, I thought, as I came out onstage. My walk-on music played, spotlights flashed, and there was some cheering from Team Max, but, as entrances went, it was a little poor.

I grabbed the microphone from Dan.

'Good luck,' he said, walking off.

I went straight into my patter. 'Do you like my outfit?' I asked. 'Pretty snazzy, huh? Wore this to an owl sanctuary the other day. Turned a few heads.'

A couple of people laughed. I could see DC Peaceful in the audience, scanning the crowd.

'I got mugged by a magician last night,' I said. 'He reached behind my ear and took my wallet.'

Nothing.

I cleared my throat and tapped the mic. 'Is this on?'

161

Someone coughed.

'Um, what did the magician's assistant say after the show? Thank you for **halving** me.'

'HA!' Daisy laughed. Otherwise, nothing. I could see Stretch looking puzzled, trying to figure out the joke.

Tough audience, I thought. Maybe a bit of crowd work?

I looked at a man in the front row. 'Where are you from, sir?' I asked.

'Surrey,' he replied.

'No need to apologise,' I said with a grin. He stared back at me. I swallowed.

In my imagination, I saw tumbleweed rolling past me.

Time for a trick, I thought. I pulled out my pack of cards and got started. I got someone up onstage and did the Pinkie Break trick. It went perfectly and the audience member gasped when I showed her her card.

The magic tricks went down a lot better than my jokes, I have to say. After all, I am pretty good at magic. The crowd warmed up as I went, and by the time we got to the wardrobe trick, people were cheering and laughing, to my great relief.

I thought I'd try just one more joke. 'I used to use a trapdoor in my shows,' I said. 'It was a stage I was going through.'

Nothing.

 163

'OK,' I said, 'Fine. No more jokes.'

A few people cheered.

'Just excuse me for a moment,' I said to the audience. 'Back in a sec.'

I opened the wardrobe door and closed it behind me. I'd been practising this a lot. I ripped the red suit off and jammed it into a cardboard box I'd left in there earlier. I wasn't going to make the mistake of tripping over the stupid thing again. Then I opened the door and walked out in my green suit.

The crowd went wild. They absolutely loved it! I got the impression they hadn't really expected much, and I'd exceeded their expectations. But I'll take it, I thought, as I bowed. Even DC Peaceful was clapping and cheering. I looked out over the crowd, waving and grinning.

Bottley the Brilliant had pulled it off!

Then my heart dropped into my boots.

At the back of the theatre stood two men. Two familiar men. One short and stocky, the other tall and thin. The Crayfish Twins.

Unbelievable!

9

Wardrobe Wobbles

My first reaction was panic. The last time I'd seen Barry Crayfish, he'd been pointing a knife at me. This wasn't like facing Bottley the Bully. The worst thing Bottley had ever done to me was stuff my head down a toilet.

The Crayfish Twins were **really** nasty,

and they had a genuine reason to hate me. I was responsible for sending them to jail in the first place. They would stuff **all** of me down the toilet, in pieces.

'Encore! Encore!' someone in the crowd shouted.

Then I remembered that I was in disguise. The Crayfish Twins didn't know it was me up onstage. Which was why they weren't actually looking at me, unlike everyone else in the theatre. They were busy scanning the crowd. I breathed a sigh of relief.

Then my heart froze once more as I saw Gary shoot out a hand to point at some seats near the front. The seats where my friends were sitting! The twins hurried down the aisle towards them. They must have recognised my friends from that day in the market. Some people had got up to leave, assuming the show was already over.

I had only seconds to stop the Crayfish Twins reaching my friends.

'You want an encore?' I yelled.

'No!' Greenjacket Dan bellowed. He frowned at me and made throat-cutting motions. 'We've got the Senior Sit-Down Stretch class here in twelve minutes.'

But I ignored him. The people who had got up sat back in their seats, and Barry and Gary Crayfish seemed unsure what

 169

to do. They shuffled to one side of the auditorium, trying to hide in the shadows, clearly having decided to wait.

'I need three volunteers!' I shouted. Dozens of hands shot up. 'You three,' I said, pointing to Team Max. 'Up onstage, please.'

Sophie looked puzzled,' but I nodded at her and gave her a **look**. She nodded back. Stretch, Daisy and Sophie came up onstage with me.

'Quick,' I said. 'In the wardrobe.'

'All of us?' Sophie asked. 'What's going on?'

'The Crayfish Twins are here,' I whispered.

I looked over to the crooks and saw that they had now climbed the stairs at the side of the stage, into the wings. They had us trapped! And DC Peaceful was sitting right there, oblivious to the danger.

We all squeezed into the wardrobe and I shut the door with some difficulty.

'I need a wee,' Stretch hissed.

'What's the plan?' Daisy asked. 'Want me to spring out and wrestle them to the stage? Cos I'll do it.'

'I'm sure you could,' I said. 'But they might be armed.'

'We need to attract DC Peaceful's attention,' sensible Sophie said. 'This is a job for the police.'

'Is there a false bottom to this wardrobe?' Stretch asked. 'Or a false ceiling? A false anything, really. I could climb through and run to get DC Peaceful.'

'By the time you got him up onstage

through the crowd, it would be all over,' I said. 'I have a much better plan.'

'What is it?'

I grinned and said, '**Stop**.'

Everything stopped. Everyone froze. Everything went deathly quiet. I shivered. My skin crawled. I hated it. But needs must. I opened the door and peered out. The crowd was sitting there, looking expectantly up at the wardrobe. Greenjacket Dan was glaring at me, hands on hips. The Crayfish Twins were glaring as well, waiting for their chance to strike.

How had they found us? The gangsters were part of a big criminal gang, I knew. Maybe they had informants in the police?

Maybe the conspiracy went right to the top? Or maybe they really had caught the domino documentary on UKTV Kids Gold 4?

I took a deep breath and felt the tingle grow in my chest. Slowly I raised a hand. The wardrobe lifted up off the stage. I walked with it, the heavy wardrobe hovering as it moved along the stage, into the wings and out into the backstage area. Then I walked it through the huge service doors at the back and all the way outside. I was growing tired. This was the longest I'd made time stop, and it was sapping my magical strength a lot! Add in the telekinesis, and I wasn't sure how much longer I could hold it.

'Sorry about this,' I said, then I tipped the wardrobe over. My frozen friends tumbled out onto the grass. Then I turned and brought the wardrobe back inside. Part of me wanted to just start time flowing and run for it, now we were clear.

But the bigger part of me was thinking about the look on the crowd's faces when the 'trick' was completed. Not to mention the fury of the Crayfish Twins. I am Max the Magnificent, after all!

Sorry, no. I was currently Bottley the Brilliant!

I put the empty wardrobe back where it had been. Normally my self-imposed rule is not to cheat when performing magic –

by which I mean I don't use my **real** magic, because that's not fair. But I thought, on this occasion, under these circumstances, it might be forgivable.

At this point, a sensible person would have gone to meet his friends outside, explain what had happened and rush off to find a responsible adult.

But I'm not a sensible person. Never have been, never will be. And what I wanted more than anything else was to see the crowd's reaction to our amazing disappearing trick. I mean, what's the point of doing magic if you don't get to see people's jaws drop? If you don't get to hear the sharp intake of breath as they realise what's just happened? If you don't get to show off a bit?

And it wasn't as if the Crayfish Twins were going to recognise me. I changed my appearance again, this time so people wouldn't recognise me as Bottley. I wanted to make myself look as dull and unmemorable as possible, so I took on the boring appearance of boring Mr Hughes, the boring maths teacher.

I took a seat in the audience to watch the show.

'Go,' I said firmly.

Greenjacket Dan waited a few seconds, then he walked over to the wardrobe. With a cross look on his face, he yanked the door open.

The wardrobe was empty.

The crowd gasped.

'WOW!' I cried loudly. 'What a trick!'

Dan peered inside. He tested the interior walls and the floor of the wardrobe, then the ceiling. Everything was solid.

He turned to the audience, held out his arms and said simply, 'They're gone.'

The crowd erupted into cheers and wild applause. I grinned and soaked it all up. I could just see the Crayfish Twins in the wings, looking furious. Then DC Peaceful came up the aisle, finally realising that he should be doing something to keep an eye on his charges, presumably.

The Crayfish Twins turned and ran. I was going to need to talk to DC Peaceful soon, but first I had to make sure my friends were OK.

'Max,' Sophie said as we hurried back to our cabins, 'thank you for getting us out of there, but please never do anything like that again.'

'How did it feel for you?' I asked.

'One moment we were all crammed together in the wardrobe,' Daisy said. 'Then we heard you say "stop". The next thing we knew, we were lying outside on the grass.'

'It was pretty scary, I'm not going to lie,' Daisy said. And if Daring Daisy was scared by something, you knew it was serious.

'What about you, Stretch?' I asked. 'How do you feel? You look really unhappy!'

'I just really need the loo,' Stretch said.

Maybe it's a bit of a blessing for Stretch that he can only ever concentrate on one thing at a time.

I had texted DC Peaceful and asked him to meet us at my cabin so we could explain what had happened. I thought we'd be safe there, and I wanted to see Lucky.

I popped into Chris's cabin, but Lucky wasn't there.

'I left him in your cabin,' Chris said. He was holding a blowtorch.

I ran up the steps and pulled out my key. But then I stopped. Something was wrong. The door was ajar.

'Lucky?' I called. But there was no scrabbling of paws. No little furry face. No one begging for bacon. The others came in behind me.

'He's gone,' I said.

'I'll check the bathroom!' Stretch said, waddling quickly towards the bathroom door.

'Maybe he escaped?' Sophie said.

'Where would he go?' I asked.

'He's a dog,' Daisy said. 'He's probably on the beach chasing gulls.'

But I knew Lucky would never have gone off on his own.

'What's this?' Daisy asked. I turned and saw her pick up a sheet of paper from the desk. She handed it to me.

'You read it,' I said.

'It says, "We got your dog.

Meet us behind the grand mall at 6 p.m. If you want him back. We just want to talk.

If you tell the police or anyone else, then you'll never see your dog again. Come alone.

Barry and Gary Crayfish."'

I gulped.

10

When All Else Fails . . .

'I still think you should call the police,'
Sophie said. 'I'm sure they have a crack
team used to dealing with this sort of
intense, life-or-death knife-edge situation.'

'They have Detective Constable Simon
Peaceful,' I pointed out. 'He's currently
dressed as Monty the Mongoose.'

'That's the last thing they'd expect,' Sophie said. 'Anyway, you were on your way to tell him you'd seen the Crayfish Twins.'

'That was before they nabbed Lucky,' I said. 'It's too dangerous now. No police.'

'You don't need police back-up when you have Team Max!' Daisy said grimly.

'We'll be there,' Sophie agreed, slightly grudgingly.

'Yeah, we got your back,' Stretch said.

'They said to come alone,' I pointed out.

'We'll stay nearby,' Daisy said. 'We'll get camouflage paint and disguise ourselves as bushes and rocks.'

'Can I be a tree?' Stretch asked.

'Of course you can,' Daisy said.

'It's fine,' I said. 'You guys just wait inside the double doors at the back of the mall. I'll grab Lucky, come through the doors and if they chase me, you can . . . I don't know. Trip them up. Stop them.'

'Perform a citizen's arrest,' Sophie suggested, her eyes gleaming.

'Good luck with that,' Daisy said. 'Look, Max, we're here for you, OK? We'll do whatever it takes to help you get away with Lucky. But how are you going to snatch him from them?'

I winked. 'I'm going to cheat.'

185

I was five minutes early, but the Crayfish Twins were already there. They had Lucky in a cage in between them.

'Max!' he yelped when he saw me. 'Get me out of here!'

'Stop barking!' Barry snapped at him.

'I tried to escape, I tried to fight, I tried to call for help. But they were too strong.'

'You were asleep, weren't you?' I asked.

'Yes, I was,' he admitted. 'Did you bring any food?'

'Come a little closer,' Barry Crayfish said. 'We won't hurt you, Max Magic.'

I stepped forward and looked at him fiercely, though I didn't feel fierce. I felt terrified. I tried to remind myself that I was Max the Magnificent. I had magical powers. I could knock them down with telekinesis, I could make an illusion to frighten them out of their minds. I could even stop time.

 187

But when you're an eleven-year-old boy facing two adults who will stop at nothing, it's hard to feel confident. Besides, I was still tired from my magical performance earlier in the day. I didn't know how much tingle I still had in me.

'Last time we were this close, a freak windstorm foiled our plans,' Barry said.

'And in June!' Gary agreed. 'You don't normally get freak windstorms in London until September.'

'Shut up, Gary,' Barry snapped.

'So, what now?' I asked, trying to stop my voice from trembling. 'Are you going to do what you tried to do last time? Attack me with a knife?'

'That's not what I want,' Barry said.

'What do you want?' I asked.

'I want what you have,' he growled.

I hesitated. What did he mean?

'You want my hat?' I asked. 'My bike? My dazzling wit and perfect fashion sense?'

'You know what I mean,' he said. 'Your powers. Your magic.'

'I can teach you how to force a card on someone,' I said, shrugging.

'Ooh, yes please,' Gary said.

'I'm not talking about stupid card tricks,' Barry said. 'I mean the real magic. The magic that lets you move things. That lets you make illusions. The magic that made that windstorm.'

'In June,' Gary repeated.

'I don't know what you're talking about,' I stuttered.

Barry narrowed his eyes at me. 'You know, I'm a bit of a magician myself,' he said. 'I can make people disappear.'

I swallowed hard.

'I've had some people watching you,' Barry Crayfish said. 'Ever since you got us locked away. They've told me some very interesting things. Shooting cans with your finger in the churchyard. Making dragons appear from out of the stage at the theatre. Casting some sort of spell on your classmate George Bottley.'

I gasped. I couldn't help myself.

'Oh yes,' Barry said with a crooked smile. 'I know who Bottley is. And I know that was you pretending to be him onstage earlier. Took me a while to figure it out. But figure it out I did.'

'How did you do that trick, by the way?' Gary asked. 'It was amazing!'

I swallowed. I had nothing to say. I wondered if this was the time to act. Stop time. Grab Lucky and just run. We could tell DC Peaceful what had happened. I didn't have much hope he'd be able to arrest two desperate criminals, but he might be able to help us get away, back to London. To safety. I was tired, but I'd only need to keep the magic going for thirty seconds.

 191

I opened my mouth, about to say the word, when Barry spoke again.

'It's something to do with that old woman's shop, isn't it?' he asked.

My breath froze in my throat.

'Now, of course I could just send my people in there anytime,' Barry went on. 'Ask them to look around the place. There might be a few breakages, unfortunately, but that's by the by. Or . . .' he continued, 'you could tell me exactly what it is we're looking for. Then we can slip in, grab it and get out. The old lady won't be bothered. There won't be no . . . breakages. If you catch my drift?'

'He's talking about vases, glasses, that sort of thing,' Gary explained. 'Maybe the odd teacup.'

'No, he's not,' I replied grimly.

'Clever boy,' Barry said. 'And a clever boy like you knows when he's beat, right? So, tell us what we're looking for in that old shop. And we'll let your little doggie go. Everyone wins.'

I thought this over. If I gave away the

 193

secret of the chest, I had no guarantee that they would stick to the bargain. They might keep Lucky. They might smash up the shop and hurt Gran anyway, just to spite me. And imagine if the Crayfish Twins got the powers of the chest. What if they could shoot firebolts, or read minds? What if they learned to stop time?!

I lifted my hand and felt the magic tingle in my chest. It was time to fight! I could zap them with my telekinesis. Send them flying.

'Hands down,' Barry said. He opened Lucky's cage and lifted him out, clutching my little dog tightly. Then he opened the flap of his coat, and with his other hand drew a long, cruel-looking knife from a scabbard on his belt.

I couldn't risk it. If I knocked Barry over, he could hurt Lucky with that knife, either accidentally or on purpose.

An illusion then. Terrify them.

A giant plant sprang out of the soil. It had huge, gaping jaws with hundreds of sharp teeth.

Gary howled and fell backwards. Lucky yowled and struggled to escape.

'It's an illusion,' Barry cried. 'Ignore it!'

The plant snapped its great jaws over Barry's head, but he hardly flinched. The plant's bite, of course, had no effect. I let it dissolve away. My powers were ebbing and I felt desperately tired. I took a deep breath. Come on, Max! I told myself. The power of suggestion, then.

'I **suggest** you –' I began.

'I suggest **you** stop talking,' Barry snapped, holding the knife closer to Lucky's neck. I stopped talking and swallowed.

Mind reading? I wasn't really sure how

that would help, but I tried to read his mind, and what I saw terrified me. He was utterly determined. He was willing to hurt Lucky or even **kill** him to get what he wanted.

So that just left one power. And presumably one he didn't know about.

'You've gone quiet, Mr Magic,' Barry grunted. 'That's not like you. Got nothing to say for yourself?'

I stared straight back at him and took a deep breath, feeling the power rising in my chest.

'I have just one thing to say,' I said.

'What's that?' he asked with a scowl.

'**Stop.**'

I wasn't sure how much time I had. I could feel what was left of my power draining away. I suspected that when it was gone, and I fell to the ground unconscious, time would start up again of its own accord, not needing me to tell it to go. I was holding back the universe, and the universe didn't need my permission to carry on. I rushed over to where the two crooks stood, frozen in the eerie silence. I gently pulled Barry's knife hand away from Lucky's neck and gently prised my poor pup out of the crook's clutches. Lucky was stiff, frozen in time along with the rest of the universe. But I gave him a quick squeeze and a kiss on the head, relieved he was safe. Or at least safe for now. I made to move away, but then I hesitated. Could I take Barry's knife away? Maybe, but I didn't feel like I had enough time. The yang of the universe was pulling against the yin of my power. The important thing was to get away – back to safety.

I turned and I ran.

As I burst through the double doors back into the mall, the spell ended without me saying anything. Noise and movement flooded back into the world, at once a relief and a reminder of the danger I was in. Lucky started in surprise and looked up at me. I winked at him and

put him on the ground so he could run.

But then I heard the doors behind me crash open.

'There he is!' I heard Barry cry. 'After him!'

I turned instinctively and saw them running at me through the crowds.

Then suddenly Daisy appeared on her bike, blocking their path. She definitely wasn't allowed to ride her bike through the mall. The Crayfish Twins slammed into Daisy's bike, and everyone went sprawling. Bystanders shouted in alarm.

'Run, Max!' Daisy shouted as she got to her feet. Barry grabbed for her, but Daring Daisy was too quick.

Leaving her bike, she darted off into
the House of Horrors. Daisy was never one
to avoid facing her greatest fears. The
Crayfish Twins seemed to consider going
after her for a moment, but then they
turned, saw me and once more gave chase.
I considered using my telekinesis to pick
up one of the massive mongoose-shaped

recycling bins and dump it on their heads, but there were too many people around for this to be safe, and I wasn't sure I had the strength. I took the opportunity to run instead.

I raced through the crowd, shouting, 'I **suggest** you get out of my way!'

And hearing the power of my suggestion, people did. But they weren't quite so inclined to let the Crayfish Twins through, and I could hear them behind me, barging into people, shouting angrily – the sorts of words that would get you a detention if a teacher caught you saying them at school.

I spotted Sophie at the door to the bingo hall. She motioned me in that direction and Lucky and I changed course, running in through the doors. Sophie slammed them behind us. 'There's another door at the far end,' she said. 'Go through there and I'll slow them down.'

I didn't wait to be told twice. I sprinted hard for the far end of the hall, weaving between the empty tables and leaping over the occasional chair left in the way. Lucky raced along at my side.

I heard the twins crash through the doors behind me. Again, I couldn't resist turning to see. They saw me, shouted furiously, and came hurtling across the wooden floor.

'Oi!' Sophie cried. The twins stopped

and looked at her. Sophie was up on the stage, next to her beloved bingo ball machine. She tipped it over.

Bingo balls scattered across the floor, bouncing and pinging about like crazy. Gary skidded, Barry slid. Both of them went over on their backsides, howling with shock.

Good old Sophie, I thought with a grin, as I turned and ran through the doors out into the sunshine.

But then I skidded to a stop.

I found myself in a small courtyard with a big gate at one side. I was in a dead end. If the gate had been open, then no problem. Presumably Sophie had expected it to be open. She was too clever not to have thought of that. But it was firmly closed, bolted shut and locked with a very large padlock.

Unbelievable!

11

The Great Escape

'What now, Max?' Lucky asked desperately.
My exhausted mind raced, trying to think
of a solution. I knew the bingo balls would
only slow the crooks down for a minute or
two.

I ran over to the lock and looked at it
carefully. I concentrated hard, trying to

see inside it, trying to figure out the lock
mechanism so I could use my telekinesis to
open it.

'Hurry, Max,' Lucky said, racing up and
down in front of the gate.

Finally, I decided to just crack the lock
open. I concentrated hard, searching for
the last traces of magic power within me.
Slowly I felt the power rise in my chest,
then . . .

The lock flew apart, a shard of metal just missing my left ear. I pulled the ruined pieces of the padlock away and grabbed the bolt to slide it across.

Then a meaty hand landed on my shoulder.

'Got you,' Barry Crayfish hissed.

'No, you haven't,' a voice said from above me. I looked up to see the extremely welcome face of Stretch. He was dangling from the top of the gate by his feet. Stretch reached one long gangly arm down. I reached up and we grabbed each other's wrists, but Barry tightened his grip on my shoulder and tried to pull me back.

Lucky leaped up, and as I grabbed him

209

with my free hand he bit Barry on the hand. The crook howled in pain and loosened his grip, allowing Stretch to haul us up, out of the clutches of the Crayfish Twins.

'Thanks, man,' I said once we were safely on the other side. 'But we still need to run. I just destroyed the padlock. They'll be through in a few seconds.' As I spoke, I heard the clank of the bolt on the other side of the door.

We ran.

We made it around the corner of the mall building before we heard the gate swing open. The Crayfish Twins wouldn't know which way we'd gone.

But where should we go? Stretch

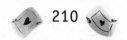

looked at me expectantly. Then I suddenly remembered I'd texted DC Peaceful earlier to tell him to meet me at our cabin. He would probably be there right now, waiting for me. DC Peaceful was hardly a tough action cop, but he was better than nothing.

'This way,' I said, pointing in the direction of the accommodation area.

'Let's go the other way and take the long way around,' Stretch said. 'They won't be expecting that.'

I nodded and we jogged back through the funfair, trying to keep a low profile and blend in with the crowds. It took us a while, but we got back to the cabin area safely enough, approaching from the back

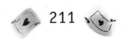

211

so we could sneak in, just in case the twins were watching the front.

I peeked around the corner. There was no sign of DC Peaceful. The one time I wanted him to show up, he was nowhere to be seen. Typical!

Then I heard a rustling from the bushes behind us. I spun to see two familiar figures stepping out from the thick foliage of a rhododendron.

Barry and Gary Crayfish.

I groaned. Did these guys never give up? I was exhausted. I had no energy for magic. I just wanted to lie down and go to sleep.

'Just tell us where the magic comes

from,' Barry said, stepping towards me. He looked as tired as I felt. Gary was puffing and panting behind his brother. 'We don't want to do this any more than you do. Just tell us what we need to know and all this goes away. I promise.'

Maybe I should just tell them, I thought. I could tell them, and then phone Gran and tell her to go somewhere safe, or maybe even tell her to destroy the chest before they arrived. Or swap it with another one or . . .

I shook my head. 'I'm not telling you anything,' I said grimly.

Barry stepped forward, a fierce look in his eyes. He pulled out his knife again,

213

the blade gleaming wickedly in the evening sunshine.

It was all over, I thought.

Then I heard a rushing, whistling sound from behind me. Barry and Gary looked above me, their eyes wide. They had half a second to look alarmed before the kite shot over my head and slammed into them at incredible speed.

The crooks went down in a tumble of limbs and kite struts and a long ribbon tail.

Just as I thought the day couldn't get any stranger, a giant mongoose burst through the bushes, screaming like a banshee, and landed on the crooks with an OOF!

The mongoose's head fell off, revealing DC Peaceful inside. He glared into Barry Crayfish's astonished face. 'You're nicked,' he growled.

12

End of the Line

Of course, Vinnie, Susie and Chris wanted us all to get the next train back home.

'What for?' I asked. 'The Crayfish Twins are behind bars again and our booking is valid to the end of next week.'

We were all sitting around a big table in the Monty's Burger Shack in the food court.

Stretch was eating a Monster Mongoose burger, which had three patties and four onion rings.

'What if there are more gangsters hanging around?' Chris said, acting all responsible. I think he felt guilty that he hadn't really been keeping an eye on us. Now he was going to overcompensate.

'There might be gangsters in the East End too,' I said. 'That's more likely, in fact.'

'The East End is full of gangsters,' Daisy added.

'And pickpockets,' Sophie added.

'And Spanish tourists,' Stretch said.

'Terribly dangerous place,' I said. 'Much safer here.'

Chris's phone buzzed on the table and he looked at the screen, which read 'Dad'.

'Well, let's let Mum and Dad decide,' Chris said.

I sighed. They would definitely want us to come home. Chris answered the call and put it on speaker.

'Hello, Chris. How is everyone?' Dad sounded worried.

'Hi, Dad,' Chris said. 'You're on speaker. There's been some excitement here. But don't worry. The police have rearrested the Crayfish Twins.'

'I know – Detective Vicky called me. She said DC Peaceful did a great job,' Dad said.

Daisy, Stretch, Sophie and I exchanged a look. While we'd all been grateful to DC Peaceful for turning up when he did, Team Max had done the hard work. Along with a magical kite of course.

'What time does your train get in?' Dad asked.

'We don't have to come back straight away, do we?' I butted in.

'Your mother and I would like you to come home,' Dad said gently.

'But the Crayfish Twins are behind bars,' I pointed out. 'We're not in danger any more.'

'It's not that,' Dad said. He paused for a moment. 'It's your gran.'

'What about her?' I asked, my voice cracking.

Vinnie and Susie looked at each other nervously. Chris swallowed.

'She's not very well,' Dad said. 'She had a fall and she's gone into hospital.'

My head swam, and I felt a weight on my chest. Sophie put a hand on my shoulder. Susie reached across the table and took my hand.

'We'll start packing,' Chris said. And I was suddenly glad he was there, being all grown-up. And Susie, and Vinny, and everyone. It's at times like these you need your family and friends around.

'There's a train leaving here at 2.35 p.m.

It'll get into Liverpool Street just before five.'

'Is Gran going to be OK?' I asked.

Dad hesitated again. 'She's getting the best possible care,' he said. 'I know she'd love to see you.'

No one spoke much on the train back. It had been an exhausting day, and I just couldn't stop thinking about Gran. I've seen hospital dramas on TV, and I know that when people say things like 'She's getting the best possible care', that isn't usually good news. What you want them

to say is something like 'She'll be fine!' or 'It's just a routine procedure'. Or 'We're just keeping her in overnight to monitor her blood pressure.'

Mum and Dad met us at the station along with Sophie, Daisy and Stretch's parents. Everyone stood around chatting and laughing like nothing had happened, until eventually I tugged on Mum's sleeve.

'Shouldn't we be going to the hospital?' I asked.

'We'll go in the morning,' she said. 'Your gran is sleeping now and visiting hours are over.'

'Is she going to be OK?' I didn't want to ask the question, because I thought I knew

223

what the answer would be, but I couldn't help myself.

Mum smiled and put her hand on my shoulder. 'She's old, Max. And she hasn't been well for some time. When old people fall, it can be quite serious.'

'Is she going to die?' I asked.

'We don't know,' Mum said. 'But she might.'

My face must have fallen, because Mum gave me a big hug. 'I'm trying to be honest with you, Max,' she said. Her voice sounded muffled with my head enveloped in her hug. 'I'm not going to tell you everything will be all right, because I just don't know.'

I nodded and wiped away a tear.

We walked the half mile or so back to the house, through the streets of the City, in the evening sunshine. Lucky was sad too. He was used to spending all day with Gran, sleeping on a comfy old armchair in a patch of sun, helping her out by testing dog-friendly biscuit treats, and protecting the shop from shoplifters, marauders and that stinky Labrador from down the street.

Dinner was lively and noisy as usual. The Mullers household never stays quiet for long, and there was lots of other news to catch up on. Dad had sold out of the helicopters and was waiting for a new batch. Mum's boss Karen had broken up with her boyfriend again. But there was a

note of worry in everyone's voices at the same time. A dark cloud hung over the table.

When it was finally time for bed, I had trouble getting to sleep even though I was completely exhausted. Eventually I dropped off around 2 a.m., with Lucky snuggled up against me, my hand resting on his side.

We couldn't all go in to see her together, so we took turns. Lucky was furious that he wasn't allowed in the hospital at all.

'We could tell them I'm an emotional support dog,' he said.

'Emotional support dogs are calm and gentle,' I pointed out.

'I'm calm and gentle!' he barked furiously.

When it was my turn, Mum asked if I wanted her to go in with me. I shook my head. I wanted to be alone with Gran. Mum gave my shoulder a squeeze and I opened the door and went in.

Gran looked tiny in the big bed. She had a tube going into her arm and her face was tired and wan, but she was awake. She gave me a weak grin. 'How was Bupkins?' she asked.

'It was great, but never mind about that,' I said. 'How are you?'

 227

'Oh, can't complain,' she said. 'The chef here is a magician. The food is **ta-da** for.'

'Gran,' I said. 'That's a terrible joke, even by your standards.'

She chuckled.

'How are **you**?' I asked again.

'It's me old ticker,' she said. 'It's nearly out of ticks.'

I didn't say anything. I knew that if I tried, the words would get all choked up and I wouldn't be able to stop the tears.

'Max,' Gran said, 'come closer.'

I sat in the chair by her bed and took her hand.

'You're going to have a wonderful long life and an exciting career,' she said. 'You have magic in you. Real magic. You know what I mean.'

Suddenly I realised that I might not get another chance to talk to her about this. 'Are you talking about the chest in the cellar?' I asked softly.

She nodded, and my heart leaped, despite everything. Gran knew! I'd suspected as much.

'I knew it was special the moment it turned up at the shop,' she said. 'I figured Arthur must have found it on his travels.'

'He did,' I said. 'We found his old diary inside.'

Gran's eyes sparkled, as if she was

imagining the places the chest must have seen.

'And did he know what was inside it?' she asked in a whisper.

I nodded. 'He thought it was some kind of spirit. A genie perhaps. Something magical and . . .' I tried to remember the word Sophie had said.

'Castanets?' I tried. 'Capricorn? Carstairs? You know, unpredictable?'

'Capricious.' Gran chuckled. 'I think the genie played a couple of tricks on you, didn't it?'

I nodded. 'Why me though? Why not you?'

'I think it has a plan for you,' Gran said.

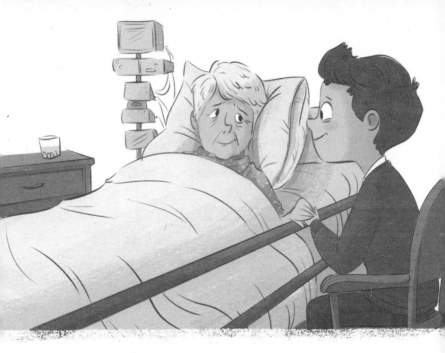

'It's almost like it's testing you. How will you use these powers? Will you use them for good, or for . . . not good?'

'I'm trying to use them in the right way,' I said. 'I don't think I always get it right.'

'None of us do, Max,' Gran said. 'But we need to keep trying.' She reached

across slowly and placed her old, thin hand against my chest.

'You have a good heart in there, Max,' she said. 'And it's strong too. I think the genie chose well.'

'But what now?' I asked. 'What does it expect me to do?'

Gran shrugged and lay back on the bed, as though the effort of moving had exhausted her. 'Why don't you ask the genie?'

I blinked in surprise. 'I can talk to it?' I asked.

'I've been talking to it,' Gran said. 'It doesn't always make a lot of sense, mind you.'

That reminded me of Lucky.

Then I remembered the day I'd come into the shop and heard Gran talking to someone in the cellar. She'd been talking to the genie?!

'How do you . . .' I paused. 'How do you, like, summon it?'

'You don't have to,' Gran said. 'Just start talking. Sometimes it talks back, sometimes it doesn't.'

'It's conspicuous,' I said.

'That's right,' Gran agreed. 'It's conspicuous.'

Dad came in then. It was time for me to go. 'I'll visit again tomorrow,' I said, looking intently at Gran. 'OK?'

'I'm not going anywhere,' Gran said.

233

'Not just yet.' Then she leaned towards me and whispered, 'I want to hear what the genie says to you.'

I had my own key for Gran's shop, so Lucky and I walked over once we'd got back from the hospital. I actually felt much better after seeing her. I'd been scared. I hadn't known what to expect. But it was just Gran: just the same as always. A bit smaller, perhaps, and paler. But still her. And she'd finally confirmed what I'd suspected for a while: that she knew about my powers. That had been amazing to hear. Gran thought there was a reason the genie had given me my powers. She thought it made sense. And that was a big relief.

I closed the door and Lucky and I went through to the back room. There was an empty teacup and a plate of biscuit crumbs on the table. I took them into the little kitchen and washed them up. Putting off the inevitable.

'Come on, Max,' Lucky said. Nervously, we walked down the stairs to the cluttered cellar.

I walked over to Arthur Andrews's chest and grasped the lid as I had done so many times before. What would happen this time? Would the genie play another trick on me?

 235

Give me another power? Or take one away?

Lucky ducked into his Safe Zone behind the table.

I held my breath and lifted the lid.

Nothing happened.

'Now what?' Lucky said.

I shrugged. 'Um . . . hello? Mr Genie?'

'Or Mrs Genie,' Lucky said.

'Sorry, Mr or Mrs Genie?' I stumbled. 'Or just . . . Genie?'

I waited. Nothing happened again.

I tried using my mind-reading power, to see if I could detect another mind in the room. Just Lucky. I frowned at him. 'How are you thinking about bacon at a time like this?'

'Part of me is always thinking about bacon,' Lucky explained.

We waited a while longer.

'Maybe we should light some candles?' Lucky suggested.

'Hmm,' I said doubtfully.

'Or sacrifice a goat?'

'Where would we get a goat from?' I asked.

'Not a real goat,' Lucky said. 'Maybe a sheep? I think Gran might have left some lamb chops in the fridge.'

'Nice try,' I said. 'But I am not giving you lamb chops.'

'This is pointless,' I said after a couple more minutes had passed. 'I'm starting to

 237

think the genie only talks to Gran.'

'Maybe you need to say "open sesame",' Lucky said. 'That's what Aladdin said.'

'Fine.' I sighed. 'But if it doesn't work, I'm out of here. **Open sesame!**'

A shimmering cloud of green and red dust formed over the chest. I yelped and fell backwards. Lucky yelped and hid.

'Seriously?!' I said. 'Open sesame?!'
The shimmer, who I guess was the genie,

made a strange coughing noise. It took me a few seconds, but then I realised it was laughter. This was its idea of a joke.

'Everyone's a comedian,' I muttered.

I waited for the genie to say something. But it didn't. Eventually, I cleared my throat and spoke. 'Are you . . . are you the genie?'

'Spirit,' the thing hissed. Its voice was the sound of sand shifting in the wind.

'What is your name?' I asked. Now I actually had the genie's attention, I couldn't think of much to say.

'No name,' the spirit replied slowly.

Then it was time to ask the important stuff.

'Do you have any bacon?' Lucky asked.

'Be quiet, Lucky,' I snapped. 'Why have you chosen to give me these magical powers?'

'Destiny,' the spirit replied, its voice crackling and dry.

'What does that mean though?' I asked. 'Everyone keeps telling me I have some great destiny, but I don't know what it is! Am I going to be a great magician? Am I going to help people? Will I be rich and famous and even more handsome than I am now? Is it something else?'

There was a long pause before the spirit answered.

'Dunno,' it said.

'What do you mean, you don't know?' I cried. This was worse than useless.

'I do not know,' the spirit said. 'Only you know.'

'What?'

'The power is in you,' it said. 'Your destiny is yours to decide.'

'I don't understand . . .' I protested.

'Tired now,' the spirit said. 'Going.' The shimmering flecks of dust compressed together and lowered back down into the chest.

'Wait!' I said. 'I have one more question.'

'Ask,' the spirit said.

'Will Gran be OK?'

 241

'She will live forever,' the spirit said. 'Time is nothing.'

'What do you mean?' I asked. 'I don't understand!'

But the spirit was gone.

'Wow,' Lucky said after a minute or so. 'That was just so . . . unhelpful.'

I sat on a dusty old pile of suitcases and tried to make sense of what had just happened.

'I think I know what the spirit was saying,' I said after a while. 'The spirit said at the start that my destiny was in my hands. And then right at the end, it said Gran will live forever and that time is nothing.'

'That's just the sort of thing characters say in a "Star Trek" episode,' Lucky said. 'It doesn't mean anything.'

'I think it does,' I replied. 'I think it means that I gained these powers for a reason. And that reason is to save Gran.'

Lucky whined. 'I'm not sure you're thinking straight,' he said. 'You can't save Gran. You're not a doctor.'

'I'm better than a doctor,' I said, hope charging through me. I looked at him and grinned. 'I'm Max the Magnificent!'

Lucky shook his head.

'Come on, Lucky,' I said. 'We have to get back to the hospital.'

'No dogs, sorry.' A security guard stopped me as I came into the hospital with Lucky trotting beside me.

'He's an emotional support dog,' I said.

The man looked down at Lucky and frowned. Lucky glared back.

'Nope,' the man said. 'Not buying it.'

'How **dare** you?' Lucky said.

'I **suggest** you change your mind,' I said to the guard.

He paused for a second, shook his head, and nodded. 'Of course, sir. Sorry to have troubled you.'

I knew which way to go now, and we walked confidently up to Gran's ward.

But the door was closed. I thought of buzzing the receptionist, but was sure they wouldn't let me in. I walked back down the corridor, thinking about what to do next.

A hospital porter walked slowly down the corridor, straight past me. I'd noticed that doctors and nurses walked quickly around the hospital, as though they were always running behind schedule. Hospital porters, on the other hand, never seemed to be in a hurry. This one waved his pass at the door to Gran's ward, opened the door and went through.

I followed him. As the door swung closed, I lifted my hand and pointed my

finger. Using my telekinesis, I held the door open, just long enough for me and Lucky to slip inside. We were in!

I walked down the quiet ward towards the bay where Gran was, but a nurse came and stood in my way.

'Visiting time is over,' she said, firmly but with a smile.

'Oh, I'm so sorry,' I said.

She walked me to the door to the ward and showed me out. As she closed the door behind us, she added, 'And there are definitely no dogs allowed in this hospital.'

'Of course,' I said. 'I'm very sorry.'

Once the door had closed, Lucky

looked up at me and shook his head. 'Come on,' he said. 'Let's go home.'

'I'm not going anywhere,' I said. 'I have a plan.'

'What's your big plan then?' Lucky asked with a sigh.

'You'll see,' I said.

I breathed in and felt the magic tingle through me. I cast an illusion, changing my appearance. But this time I wasn't George Bottley.

My clothes changed from jeans and a T-shirt to hospital scrubs. I even added a stethoscope for the sake of appearances.

'That's not bad actually,' Lucky said grudgingly.

 247

'I haven't finished yet,' I said. 'Now it's your turn.' I concentrated again. Tingle time!

Lucky grew and stood up on his hind legs. His fur, or most of it, disappeared, and was replaced with the navy-blue uniform of a hospital porter.

I looked at him, slightly unnerved to see a human version of Lucky. Somehow he still looked a bit dog-like, with bushy whiskers and slightly furry ears.

'Why can't I be a doctor as well?!' he protested.

'Porters perform an extremely valuable role in the health service,' I pointed out. I banged on the ward door. The nurse came to open it, looking like she was about to yell at me. But then she caught sight of me and blinked in surprise.

'Oh!' the nurse cried. 'I'm so sorry, Dr . . .' she peered at my new name badge, 'Mullers. I thought you were . . .' Then she looked over at Lucky, taking in his rather hairy appearance. She frowned. Then she shook her head and looked back at me.

'Is your pass not working?' she asked, pointing to the access panel that opened the door.

'Er, no,' I said. 'Very annoying. I blame the, er . . . government.'

'What about . . . his?' she asked,

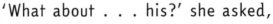

 249

looking over at human Lucky, whose name badge read 'Buster McKinley'.

Lucky shook his head.

'He's here to help me lift a patient,' I said.

The nurse hesitated. I think she could tell something wasn't quite right, but she couldn't put her finger on it. But the illusion held, and she let us in.

'Don't worry, nurse,' I said confidently. 'I know where I'm going.'

'Good work, nurse,' Lucky added. 'Carry on.'

This time she stared at Lucky with even greater puzzlement. Then I realised that though Lucky now looked like a human, he

still didn't **sound** like a human. At least,
not to anyone apart from me. This hairy
porter had just barked at her.

'He doesn't speak very good English,' I
said hurriedly.

'Where's he from?' the nurse asked.

'He's Alsatian,' I replied, then strode
on, Lucky trotting along behind me. We
went into Gran's ward and slipped inside
the curtains. I let the illusion fall, not
wanting to alarm Gran. I became me again,
and Lucky turned back into dog form.

Gran looked like she was asleep, but
when Lucky jumped up onto the bed she
opened her eyes and smiled at him. 'I
didn't think I'd see you again, my old

 251

friend,' she said. She raised a hand slowly and laid it on Lucky's head.

'How are you feeling?' I asked Gran.

'Like my batteries are running out,' Gran said, as she scratched Lucky's ears.

'Visiting time is over,' she went on. 'How did you get in?'

I grinned. 'Just a little subterfuge.'

'Did you speak to the genie?' she asked.

I nodded.

'And?'

'I think I know why he gave me my powers,' I said.

'Oh, really?'

'Yes. I think I'm supposed to help people. I think I'm supposed to save people. And I'm going to save you, Gran.'

She looked at me for a long time. Then she smiled sadly. 'Oh, Max,' she said. 'You can't save me. My time is up.'

'But it doesn't have to be,' I said. 'The genie said something about time. And the last power it gave me was the ability to stop time. Don't you see? I can stop time so that you don't die.'

'**That's** your plan?' Lucky asked, staring at me. 'That's **terrible**.'

'But what good would that do?' Gran asked. 'Then you'd be sitting around doing nothing. If you stop time, you can't live your life.'

'But, but . . .' I spluttered. 'Maybe I

 253

can stop time long enough for you to get better, then start it up again. Or, I don't know. I haven't really thought it through.'

'You don't say,' Lucky muttered.

'Max,' Gran said, 'you have to let me go. You can't stop time. At least not forever.'

Tears stung my eyes. I knew she was right. Stopping time exhausted me. I couldn't fight against the whole universe. Not for long, anyway. And even if I was able to maintain the time stop, what would I do then? No noise, no movement, no life. What was the point of that?

'The show must go on,' Gran whispered.

'But not without you,' I murmured. 'Not without you.'

'I'll still be there,' Gran said. 'In your heart. In your memory. That's the real magic, Max.'

I cried. I couldn't stop it any more than I could stop Gran from dying.

'You can do all the tricks in the world,' Gran went on, 'but real magic comes from the heart. We can't live forever, but we can survive in other people's memories, as long as we touch their hearts while we're alive.'

I perched on the edge of the bed, tears running freely now, and gave her a gentle hug, worried I would crush her; she felt so tiny and frail. That must be what the genie had meant when it told me Gran

 255

would live forever. She would go on living in our memories and in our hearts.

She whispered in my ear, 'You're going to be magnificent, Max.'

13

The Show Goes On

One month later

'What's going to happen to the shop?' Daisy
asked. We were in the churchyard, standing
in front of the newest gravestone in the
yard. Just a stone's throw from Gran's old
shop. And in the area she'd lived her whole
life.

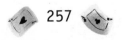 

'Mum's going to keep it running for now,' I said. 'She's finally quit her job at the hospital, so she has some time on her hands.'

Stretch placed his pink teapot on Gran's grave. 'I've drunk thousands of cups of tea in my life,' he said. 'But your gran's were always the best.'

Daisy added a brownie. 'I baked these myself,' she said. 'They're not as good as hers of course.' Then she glared at Lucky. 'That's for Gran,' she warned. 'Keep your paws off it.'

Lucky looked hurt. And hungry.

Sophie bent down and slipped a folded piece of paper torn from her Business Book

under the teapot. 'It's a poem,' she said.
'I wrote it for your gran. She was always
very kind to us.'

'Do you want to read it out?' I asked.

She shook her head. Then she looked at
me. 'Didn't you bring something to leave
on the grave? I thought you said you were
bringing flowers?'

I grinned, reached into my sleeve and
pulled out a big, bright bouquet.

Sophie sighed. 'Do you never stop?'

'Nope,' I said. 'Someone very clever
told me once that the show must go on.'

'That was me!' Lucky said.

'It was Gran!' I replied.

'I said it first,' Lucky muttered.

 259

I bent and placed the flowers against the gravestone, next to the teapot, the brownie and Sophie's poem.

I looked up and read the inscription. For once the letters and words stood out nice and clear for me.

HERE LIES
MARGARET ETHEL MULLERS
LOVING MOTHER AND GRANDMOTHER.

NOW FOREVER REUNITED

WITH HER HUSBAND JAMES,

BECAUSE YOU CAN'T

BEAT A GOOD DOUBLE ACT.

I stood. 'Come on. Let's go and get some ice cream.'

As we walked off, I thought I heard the hiss of the genie speaking to me. But it was only dry leaves being blown by the wind.

Gran had left the chest to me in her will. Mum and Dad had thought that was odd. Why had she given me a mouldy old chest from her basement?

I didn't explain. How could I explain that Gran had given that chest to me because she wanted me to carry on exploring the world of magic, the mysteries of the unknown? And maybe she wanted me to get out of (and into) a few scrapes along the way.

Because the show must go on.

And because how else do you become magnificent?

Become a magician with Stephen Mulhern

Scan this QR code to learn brand-new magic tricks!

⭐ **Step-by-step instructions**
⭐ **UNBELIEVABLE magic tricks**
⭐ **Tips from Stephen!**

How to 'Force' a Card

Boggle people's minds with this simple trick! All you need is a deck of cards, a table and a copy of Max Magic: The Incredible Holiday Hideout . . . *and you have one of those already!*

STEPHEN'S TOP TIP!

Make sure you do Step 1 and 2 before performing the trick.

1 Find the Ace of Spades in a pack of cards.

Place it on top of the pack, face down.

 Ask a friend to pick a number between 1 and 10.

 Say, 'Now I'm going to ask you to choose a card from the deck, and I will use magic to read your mind and know what your card is!'

5 Demonstrate what your friend needs to do, by dealing the same number of cards as the number they chose into a new pile.

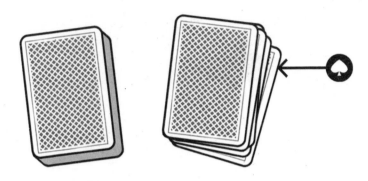

Steps 4 and 5 are to **distract** your friend as you set up the trick, by pretending that you are showing them what to do.

6 Put the dealt cards back on top of the deck. You have now made sure the Ace of Spades is in the right place for later!

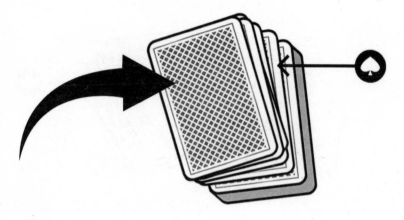

7 Give the pack of cards to your friend and ask them to deal the same number of cards into a separate pile, just like you did.

8 Ask them to turn over the top card of the smaller pile without showing you.

9 Say to them, 'It's time to reveal your card!'

10 Flick through the animation in the corner of this book with your friend to reveal their card!

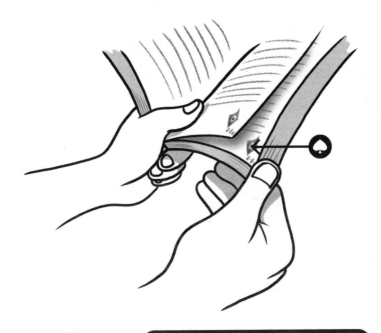

Take your time flicking through the pages so your audience doesn't miss the surprise.

Dress up as Max Magic!

YOU WILL NEED:

1. Normal clothes
2. Playing cards
3. A top hat

Optional:
Lucky the dog!

Don't forget to share your **unbelievable** costume on social media
and tag @StephenMulhern & @PiccadillyPress! **DOOSH!**

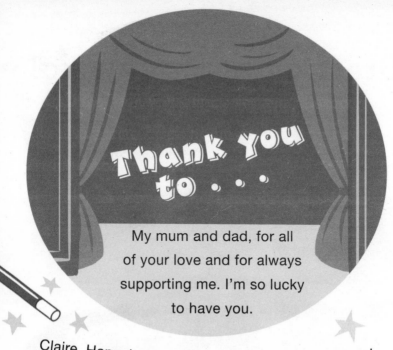

Thank you to . . .

My mum and dad, for all of your love and for always supporting me. I'm so lucky to have you.

Claire, Hannah, Matt, Millie, Amanda, and all of YMU for all of your hard work and support.

Jamie, Susie, Chris and Vince, for everything!

To Stephen Williams Jr – thank you for all you do!

Tom, it's a pleasure to work with you. What an amazing journey we've been on.

Ruth, editor extraordinaire – special thanks for always being so brilliant.

Begoña, you've captured Max like no one else could!

Everyone at Bonnier Books UK, especially Ruth, Talya, Aimee, Dom, Katie, Charlotte, Emma, Amber, Eloise, Jess, Kate and Steph. You've been incredible every step of the way! Big thanks to Nigel for your great layouts.

The biggest thanks goes to you, the reader of this book! Thanks for embracing Max and I hope he's brought as much magic into your life as he has into mine.

Tom Easton has published more than forty books for readers of all ages. He has written books about vampires, pirates, teenage girl boxers and teenage boy knitters (not all in the same book). He lives in Surrey with his wife and three children. You can find out more about him on Twitter @TomEaston

Begoña Fernández Corbalán was born and raised in a small town in Spain. As a child she loved to draw, and after finishing a degree in Fine Arts, she specialised in illustration. She works with watercolour, gouache and pencil as well as illustrating digitally.